WAR Baby

A Ruach Elohim Parable

DR. GEORGETTE V. PRIME-GODWIN

WAR Baby
A Ruach Elohim Parable
Copyright ©2018 by Georgette V. Prime-Godwin

All Scripture references are from the New International Version, (NIV) and/or New American Standard, (NAS) © 1973, 1978, 1984 by International Bible Society unless otherwise noted. Used by permission of Zondervan. All rights reserved. [Biblica] King James Version (KJV) Public Domain.

HOV Publishing a division of HOV, LLC.
www.hovpub.com
hopeofvision@gmail.com

Cover Design: HOV Design Solutions
Editor: Bettye Walker
Proofreader: Judith Banks

Visit the Author Dr. Georgette V. Prime-Godwin at:
www.warbabybook.com
www.godwininternational.org

For more information about special discounts for bulk purchases, please visit www.hovpub.com

ISBN 978-1-942871-34-7
Library of Congress Control Number: 2018943213

10 9 8 7 6 5 4 3 2 1

Printed in the United States of America

The crowd standing there heard it and said it had thundered. Others said that an angel had spoken to Him. In response, Jesus said, "This voice was not for My benefit, but yours [...] Then Jesus told them, "You are going to have the light just a little while longer. Walk while you have the light, before darkness overtakes you. Whoever walks in the dark does not know where they are going. Believe in the light while you have the light, so that you may become children of light." — John 12:29-30, 35-36a, NIV

ENDORSEMENTS

The storyline grips at your emotions and brings to the surface a spiritual element that will cause the reader to reflect on the long-term impact of their own decisions—at the same time the plot will keep the reader eager to read the next page, and just as you think you know what's next, it goes to an even deeper element. Not to give it away but the end will leave you in deep thought."

The Honorable Dennis P. Lister, J.P., M.P.
Speaker of The House of Parliament, Bermuda

Intriguing, insightful and impactful! These are the three cardinal words that I have carefully chosen to describe the prolific thoughts and skillful penmanship of Dr. "G". From the introductory sentence in chapter one and maiden power thought in that same chapter to the final sentence in chapter thirteen this fictional tale and well-crafted novel will captivate the thirsty longing of one's intellectual imagination. For those curious minds that enjoy suspense and relish in intrigue this book "War Baby" is a must read for you. Need I say anymore, I now invite you to sample for yourself and enjoy this thoughtful presentation and be blessed as you read the skillful work of Dr. "G" entitled, "War Baby."

Rev. Dr. Lloyd E. Duncan
Administrative Bishop and Pastor
New Testament Church of God, Bermuda

In her novel, War Baby, Pastor Prime-Godwin speaks from her heart and her history to share a new Christian parable. She calls us to take on the shield of God's strength to wage our personal and collective wars against the powers in this world that fight to steal our opportunity to rise above mediocrity and live blessed lives in God's light.

Jan DeMasters, PhD, RN
President & CEO
Well Advised Consulting, LLC
Chesterfield, MO

ACKNOWLEDGEMENTS

A very special thank you to The Honorable Dennis P. Lister, J.P., M.P., *Speaker of the House of Parliament*, Rev. Dr. Lloyd E. Duncan, Administrative Bishop and Pastor of *New Testament Church of God*, Jan DeMasters, PhD, RN, President and CEO of Well *Advised Consulting, LLC* and Holley Richardson, CEO of *Richline Solutions* for their tremendous support on this exciting project.

To my family, both physical and spiritual, thank you for your continued prayers, words of encouragement and affirmation of this project.

To Yahweh, who is always present and accessible to me, in you I have placed all trust. To God be the glory and thank you!

TABLE OF CONTENTS

FOREWORD

Dr. Georgette V. Prime-Godwin has penned a powerful reminder to each of us that it is the unexamined life that allows people to become needless casualties of spiritual war.

This is an exploration of the great conflict going on between good and evil within the spiritual realm, and how it unfolds and proliferates. It doesn't unfold due to lack of understanding the Word of God, but due to non-diligence. The author writes, "fight the war against mediocrity, as it is that evil that will consume your soul and personal potential." Here mediocrity describes the tendency of human beings to be *relationally mediocre* in the sense of not understanding the gifts in another and therefore overlooking the very tools given to each of us designed to be effectively used in terminating the plans of the enemy.

Spiritual warfare takes a front and center place in this book. In it you will learn that something as simple as an in-depth conversation leads to the communication, or in this case the interpretation of dreams, that could lead to effective intervention, and efficient spiritual warfare strategy—bringing deliverance and a shift in the trajectory of destinies.

Dr. Prime-Godwin is a powerful, creative and thought-provoking writer; a drum major who courageously beats the drum of spiritual sensitivity that summons us to a place where we can hear the sound of heaven that transforms us from the spiritual stagnant to proactive catalysts of change.

This book represents the unexplored inner conflict of those who march through life with fractional smiles and fully broken hearts to the discordant sound of pain. It further explores the twisted wreckage and ruined lives that can result due to the unexamined interconnectivity as few truly recognize there is a profound relational, communication-based work that is often overlooked in our approach to spiritual warfare. This is because we don't recognize the value of excavating the spiritual gifts and dynamics of being authentic and whole individuals. These spiritual gifts, when examined have the power to bring greater understanding, fortification, and expansion to the Kingdom of God. However, if left unexplored, they allow for spiritual blind spots that act as portals of access to the enemy of our soul.

This page-turning parable guarantees a return on your investment of time and energy. It is also an investment in the splendid life we can attain in Christ when we decide to spend less on external trappings of wealth and success and more on inner-healing, spiritual growth and development.

Dr. N. Cindy Trimm

Life-Strategist, Author, Humanitarian

PREFACE

Intertwined at the door stands both mediocracy and broader more distinctive opportunities. And yet, we choose to climb the wall of mediocrity and dance around the periphery of opportunity. This multifaceted mystery consumes the soul and personal potential. Blame is placed on a vindictive colloquy hidden behind a teasing gesture, the lack of parental teaching and guidance, past encounters and a deliberate stubbornness—all of which forces an evading displacement of all available methods.

Jesus said, "This voice [this sound] was not for My benefit [trajectory] but yours;"[1] meaning that the time has come for all humanity to embrace a universal trajectory of par excellence—a trajectory that propels men and women into greatness so all can become sons and daughters of the Light.

There is a society that articulates that they are part of *the called* but can only hear the claps of thunder while the Holy Spirit is audibly speaking. There are also people who reside beyond the boundaries of being *called* and infuse a belief on *the called,* obstructing the ear to the trajectory sound of par

---

[1] John 12:29-30, NIV

excellence. Both are doomed to reside in the sphere of mediocrity.

ABOUT THE AUTHOR

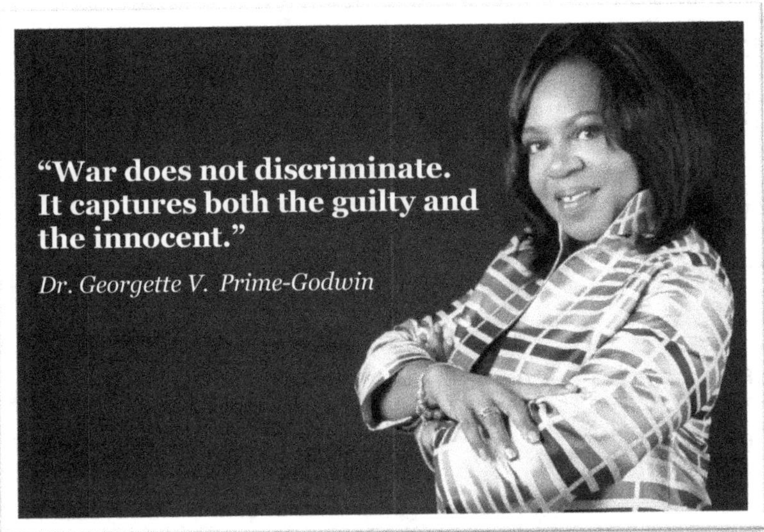

Dr. Georgette V. Prime-Godwin is an accomplished facilitator of spiritual formation, organizational leadership and business management for over 20 years. An Author and Certified Professional Life Coach, she has earned the respect of senior executives, youth and clergy personnel, having the uncanny ability to translate everyday life experiences into literal language that empowers and transforms her audiences.

Her mantra, "tiller of the earth," supports exchanges that stimulate an introspective philosophy, combined with depths of spiritual understanding, humor and personal candor—all of which are extraordinary gifts and key attributes to fueling a relaxed but attentive rapport with her participants.

A native of the beautiful Islands of Bermuda, Rev. Dr. Prime-Godwin holds a Bachelor of Science in Organizational Leadership and Management from Regent University in Virginia Beach, Virginia, a Masters of Divinity in Pastoral Leadership from Payne Theological Seminary in Wilberforce, Ohio, an Honorary Doctorate of Divinity and Chaplaincy from CICA University and Seminary in Jamaica, New York, as well as a Certified Professional Life Coach Designation from the Life Coach Institute in Orange County, Florida.

INTRODUCTION

War is an intrinsic and inflammatory position for acquisition, whether it involves a retrieval of personal possession by force, a position of headship, or to determine a tactic to undergird the economy. War can present a contest carried out by force of a nation against or for another nation, and leadership against headship bringing with it many casualties to include both the guilty and the innocent.

War is an authority to promote the sovereignty of God to mankind for the protection of a chosen group of people. War establishes a place of humility between God and humanity. War is beneficial to secure and redirect rightful ownership, while displacing those that operate in corruption.

War is evitable, yet when engaged it will stretch beyond nations, nestling itself within the bowels of one's persona as it matriculates weaponry of mass destruction. The destruction that will cause the strongest of personalities to submit to mediocrity, a family to turn against each other, and an institution of affluence to exploit its patrons.

War is without prejudice, for it is an action fueled by the personalities of those that will implement the initiative. It can engulf the actions of a subtle and brilliant mind that is yet to be demarcated by the values and truth determined by parental, educational and spiritual disclosure.

War transcends in a natural progression, arresting the culture that embraces it as a means to an end. A cultural understanding that embraces conflict as a position of harmony is an eccentric view and one that gains an unearned support by a premise of artificial entitlement.

NOS ZJILEA

War can drop in your lap at any time. You do not need to seek after it or engage it. It simply presents itself unexpectedly, without notice and with seemingly no way out of it. I marvel at other people's philosophies and what they deem to be important for success. But as for my life, I would describe it as a closed book, one too full to take on anything else and yet too voluminous to let go of the lessons learned. This was the extent of my philosophy about life until I heard the voice of God in a clap of thunder.

Become a student to the sound in the clap of thunder. It is here that you will hear His voice and discover the real you.

My name is Daniel Ophillon Schmartz, II, a fourth-generation descendant of Schmartz men who were all war veterans. My great-grandfather, Corporal Ophillon Geralzd Schmartz, served in the 1908 war against the Balinese rebels. My grandfather, Corporal Geralzd Schmartz volunteered for one term in the 1940 Indonesian National Revolution. By 1949 the war had ended and my grandfather left his native country of Saba, in the Caribbean Netherlands, for a new and safer life free of war.

Saba is nestled on the seacoast of the beautiful and untamed Caribbean Sea just east of Puerto Rico and the Virgin Islands. Influenced by Dutch Caribbean culture, it is the smallest of three municipalities of the Dutch Caribbean. It was a very close-knit community and as with most close-knit communities it denounces the opportunity for expansion, while promoting a repetitive and stagnated environment for its citizens. As such, it was everyone's dream to move to greener pastures even though relocating did not always afford such opportunities for everyone.

My father, Daniel Ophillon Schmartz, I, was born on August 12, 1941. Shortly thereafter, the family migrated to this great nation called the United States of America, taking up residency in Pella, Iowa. Pella is approximately 43 miles southeast of Des Moines, Iowa. My father was the younger of two siblings. His older brother was a casualty of war and, therefore, Pella was a welcomed change as a country without the visible scars of war. Life in Pella was tranquil for the soul, flaunting a rural landscape of Dutch architecture styles and colored with the same traditions and culture.

My momma, Thedra Grazina Belterre, was born April 15, 1938. She migrated to Pella from Bonaire with her Aunt Sybie ("Maezda Sybille Belterre Gurhart") and Uncle Sammie ("Samuel Cruz Delmonte Gurhart"). My momma's parents died tragically when she was a little girl when the cargo ship, the *Georgiana,* sank off the coast of Rincon in the Caribbean Sea. My momma would often share stories from her childhood:

"Daniel, did you know your Grandpa Theodore knew how to delicately extract pollen from the Jasminum plant to make perfume?"

Pretending I had never heard the story before I said, "Really momma? What was the name of the perfume again?"

"GraZina!" she responded. Did you know I was named after the perfume?"

Appearing shocked, I replied, "Momma! You were named after a perfume?"

We both would giggle over the conversation before momma finally turned serious. Staring off into the distance as if reminiscing on the past, she would say, "Daniel, you can accomplish anything with hard work and dedication to your dream. Your grandparents made a great team. Grandpa Theodore was responsible for the manufacturing and your Granny Bella handled the administration of the business. They perfected the process of extracting pollen from the Jasminum plant and were planning to establish a manufacturing plant in Rincon (a part of the Dutch

Caribbean) when the Georgiana sank during a fluke storm. The distance between the two was a mere twenty-two miles by sea. There were no survivors and the ship was never recovered."

Grandma Bella and Aunt Sybie were sisters. They were affectionately known as the *Belterre* girls. The wealth established by their parents went up in smoke during the Great Recession of the Dutch Caribbean in 1940. Aunt Sybie and momma would always come together and reminisce about the family's legacy so momma would never forget her heritage. In turn, momma would retell the Belterre history to me as I sat listening intently from one of the easy chairs:

"Daniel," momma said, "Your grandparents were very influential people and well respected in their community. As astute business people they always assisted those who demonstrated an interest in how to increase their wealth. Since Bonaire was an island, it posed many opportunities for the importation of products like fine linens, leather and household items to the island. But Bonaire was an expensive place to live and without the means of exportation, the people of Bonaire were easily divided into financial groupings. There were basically only two socio-economic structures—the haves and the haves not.

———————

Make serving others a priority, only then will your needs be met.

____

Grandpa Theodore was determined to break those barriers as he felt the economy should be shared equally, especially with those who worked earnestly. Grandpa's business, Le Perfumé, discovered how the pistil from the Jasminum plant could be delicately extracted. He dedicated many years perfecting the extraction process. Le Perfumé provided employment for the residents of Bonaire and it was there that the GraZina fragrance was born. The success of Le Perfumé opened the door for manufacturing plants throughout the Caribbean Dutch provinces. Bonaire had a strong voice and work acumen and had proven equality for all her citizens. Bonaire had an export item and process ready to share with all the neighboring islands. But then they died and then the great recession of 1940 would erase everything they had built together."

There was a look of great disappointment in momma's eyes as if she tried to turn back the hands of time.

"So, momma, tell me again how you and dad met?" Daniel asked.

Momma was always methodical in her response. She would say to me, "I will but first things first Daniel! You must never forget your heritage. Our family worked hard and consistently for every accomplishment they achieved. They left behind a legacy for me…a legacy which I now leave to you, son."

All the families in Pella were from at least one of the municipalities of the Dutch Caribbean territories, such as Bonaire, Sint Eustatius or Saba. My momma was a native of the island of Bonaire located on the eastern boarder off the coast of Venezuela and part of the ABC Islands. When her Aunt Sybie and Uncle Sammie migrated to Pella, Iowa in 1959, momma was just twenty-one years old. She always blushed when telling the story of how she and my dad met.

"When I saw your dad, oh my, my heart skipped a few beats! The first time I saw him was when I attended the Nos Zjilea with your Aunt Sybie and Uncle Sammie. When we saw each other for the first time, our eyes locked and I knew in my heart that he was the one! During the Nos Zjilea, you could find an infusion of Saban culture—from arts and crafts displays to music and lots of delicious food. The atmosphere was always electric!"

The look on momma's face was nostalgic. She was a great story teller and there was something about the impassionate way she told her stories that enveloped me into the experience. I could literally listen to her for hours at a time:

"Your dad had a body that any woman would dream of lying next to!" Momma said.

Grimacing over the idea of my parents being together, I said, "Oh momma! Just when I was really enjoying the story!"

"Daniel," she said affectionately, "You are going to have a body stature just like your dad when you grow up!"

My cheeks and hair were inflamed with such embarrassment that I was convinced they had merged into a single shade and color of red. Momma seemed to shrug it all off, continuing her recollection of my dad's introduction and courtship:

"He walked over to me and asked, 'May I have this dance?' His voice was so soothing and I folded myself into his arms as we danced the night away. A year later and he had proposed to me. I said yes and we have been happily married ever since. Your dad was adamant about getting married. Desirous of nothing fancy or flashy, he simply wanted to go to the courthouse and get married. On the other hand, I had always dreamed of a garden wedding and a garden wedding it was! Lake Red Park was the venue, with silhouettes of mountain terrains as a backdrop, tall evergreens cascading throughout the valley and sounds of nature melodically breaking the deathly silence in the air."

Each time momma shared the experience, I could almost imagine myself being there. "Daniel," she continued in her soft contralto voice, "Everyone in Pella pitched in and decorated all the tents and chairs. It looked like a miniature Nos Zjilea. It was a beautiful stoically hot day in July and I was a traditionally beautiful bride on that Monday, July 10, 1961. I wore my mother's wedding dress—a beautiful yet simple off–white, satin lace shiniel (midi) dress. I was holding a bouquet of freshly cut wildflowers and I had two attendants. Your dad's cousin, Belquest, served as the man of honor. By the time we said our vows, the sun was setting behind the mountain tops and we became Mr. and Mrs. Daniel Ophillon Schmartz, I."

Momma had a glow about her that permeated her entire being. I remember thinking to myself, "Maybe the same for me one day." She went on to share how the newly wedded couple settled in Pella, Iowa for several years prior to moving to Wyandanch, New York. Now miles away from their families, both families seemed genuinely disgruntled over the idea of my parents moving to New York. Siding with my dad, my mom defended my dad's decision, insisting that there were more job opportunities in New York than Iowa. Of course, my dad had a loftier reason for moving. He was convinced that the farther away he could get from my grandpa (his father), the sooner he would be free of the "war-like" mindset that plagued the Schmartz family culture.

August 12, 1963 marked a significant turning point in the Schmartz home in that my sister, Deborah Thedra Grazina Belterre Schmartz, was born in the Wyandanch Metropolitan Hospital. She was a small framed, beautiful light brown skinned baby girl with dark brown eyes and hair, weighing just over 6lbs, 10oz. Her coloration became a bone of contention for my father given that both of my parents were milky white in skin color. My dad had dark hair and eyes but was unquestionably fair skinned. As such, he relentlessly accused my momma of having an extramarital affair—something that my momma vehemently denied given that she deeply loved my father. As a point of fact, my grandpa was a Caucasian man and my granny was a beautiful chocolate brown Caribbean woman. Even though my dad was privy to this truth, he never once contemplated the possibility that my sister's skin color might have been passed down through the genealogy of the family through my granny. The ongoing debate over my sister's validity as my father's child added an undue strain and dimension to my parent's marital dynamics.

In 1965, a short few years after my sister Deborah was born, my dad enlisted in the U.S. Army. During his tenure, he obtained the rank of Corporal, serving in the Vietnam War until 1971. In 1973, my dad briefly came home on sabbatical during the Christmas holidays. Shortly after returning to duty, he was commissioned to Cambodia for intel, only to be discharged in the early part of 1978 due to a severe injury during a routine drill practice. My dad was an exceptional officer while serving his country and was well respected among his military peers. He acquired the reputation of being a man of high esteem and one that demonstrated the caliber of character everyone aspired to. He returned from war a well decorated Corporal and hero but a man with a severe case of PTSD ("post-traumatic stress disorder"). Our home was never the same.

Throughout the Schmartz ancestry, the story of war was always clearly articulated. There was something in the fight and combativeness of war that seemed to provide a sense of freedom from everything that war represented. The family's motto was "one must fight in order to be free." I interpreted this to mean that it was an honor to serve so others might be exempt (free) from the contests of war, carried on by the force of arms and the subsequent clutches of imprisonment.

I was the first to break tradition with the Schmartz legacy of war in that I never enlisted or had any exposure to the military or war. Still, I found myself engaged in a type of inner struggle and war that left me feeling imprisoned; weakened by an imposed hostility without having any contact or familiarity to war. The momentum caused by it, kept me spiraling out of control. I heard a preacher say once, "Life's instruction comes in the clap of thunder." It was in the clap of thunder that I first heard the words, "You are predestined for greatness!" But what did it all mean? My life showed no evidence of greatness. How can one be great when they are controlled and impaired by the volume of the struggle and unable to find the switch that terminates all outside and conflicting noises?

LINES ARE DRAWN

I was raised a Baptist; and as a Baptist, I experienced all the nuances and trimmings associated with the Baptist faith. Despite my ties to my faith, I still felt as though I was going through my own personal hell—a type of hell that confirmed that God was not a part of the Schmartz family legacy. Even still, momma encouraged my sister Deborah and me to attend Sunday School and the Sunday worship services every week.

The first sermon I recall that touched my heart was entitled, *Forgiveness Is Healing for The Soul.* I vividly remember momma patting me on the knee as if to confirm that the message was especially scripted for me. My sister Deborah (or "Deb" as I used to call her) was rarely engaged in the service and made it a point to sit several pews away from momma just to spite her. Deb was naturally funny and a total blast to be around. But whenever my dad came home, she would always run and hide. I asked her once why she always ran from our dad but she never answered me. She simply cried a lot and I learned never to ask her that question again.

I remembered the stories momma told and how she and dad got hitched. The man that momma spoke so passionately about was not the man I knew. I wanted him to be my hero and friend, someone who loved me and protected and cared for our family. What I got instead was this vile volatile person who was unscrupulous in his behavior towards me, my momma and my sister. I later found out that he consistently molested Deb sexually from the time she was fifteen years old. And he always made a point of engaging me in venomous conversations that raped me of my self-esteem, destroying my inner-man.

**Never welcome dishonest conversation.
It will arrest your soul.**

The irony of it all is momma told me I was born in a taxicab—on November 15, 1975—somewhere between our home on 1715 Blossom Avenue and the Wyandanch Metropolitan Hospital. I weighed a hefty 11 lbs., 13 oz. Momma referred to me as "her big happy bundle of joy!" Due to my size, she could not produce enough milk to feed me so around eight weeks old she began feeding me Pablum. By the time I was six months old, I was eating whatever food she prepared for the family, albeit chopped up finely so I could digest it. At age two, I was already two and a half feet tall and weighing 52 lbs. Momma loved kissing me on my cheeks. "Daniel," she would say, "your cheeks are like double-sized marshmallows brushed with a hint of strawberries!"

I was a big toddler and a big kid for my age—a trait which I was teased and bullied for all throughout my school years. I was also the youngest. My sister, Deb, was born almost twelve years before I was conceived. She was conceived two years before dad enlisted in the U.S. Army. The time my dad spent away in Cambodia was the happiest of times for Deb and my mom. By the time he returned, Deb was fifteen years old and everything had changed, especially her physical appearance. I nicknamed Deb "war baby" because her entire life became embroiled with a war she could never win. Our home became a reflection of the entanglements of war; and the conflicting environment of an abusive, post-traumatic, alcoholic father versus momma who tried desperately to convert the battlefield into a home and refuge for her family.

Due to our age difference, Deborah was very protective of me and would encourage me to play upstairs in the attic or anyplace where my dad could not reach. On one occasion, I recall him reaching to hit my sister because of her fierce defiance against him. Momma immediately stepped between the two of them and his wrath resulted in him slapping momma around like a rag doll. For as long as I could remember, my dad would come home drunk and beat momma. If he caught me watching, he would abruptly stop, blaming his behavior on the war. "It's that damn war," he would shout. Of course, I never did understand why he chose to place the blame on the war, when he stopped serving in the military shortly after I was born.

Tuesday, July 10, 1985 is a date that is etched in my mind forever. For one, it was one of the hottest days on record for New York. The temperature had reached a blazing 104°F. It was my parent's anniversary but not a time of celebration because dad's drinking made him more violent than I care to remember. There was little money to go around, which meant that momma had to take on a few odd jobs in the neighborhood just to keep Deb and I fed. With it being so hot and with no air-conditioning in the home, the only thing momma had to do on laundry day was to hang the laundry out on the back porch. In less than an hour everything was baked completely dry. More importantly, this date is significant because it was the day when Deb planned an escape from this war-torn situation:

"Momma," Deb said, "You promised when Daniel was old enough we would move out of this house. So, when are we moving?"

Momma's response appeared to take an eternity to answer, as if she was trying to contemplate all the possible repercussions from such a drastic move.

"Sweetheart, we can't move right now because we can't afford it."

Deb was relentless. Moving closer to momma's side, Deb gently took momma's hand in her hand, holding it firmly. "But momma, we can't afford to stay. If we don't move someone is going to die in this house!"

Gazing towards the doorway of our small kitchen, momma noticed me peaking around the corner. "Come here son, please."

I loved my momma. She was the kindest person ever and from a strong Dutch heritage. Her skin was nearly milky-white in color. Her hair was reddish-brown in color and she had these huge translucent hazel eyes. Her hands, although calloused from hard labor, were gentle to touch. I ran to her, nestling my head into her breast just to hear the melodic and rhythmic beats of her heart. With tears running down her face, momma said:

"Daniel, momma is tired. I want you to go with your sister somewhere safe, far away from this house and me."

"Oh no, momma, we are all leaving together," Deborah proclaimed. I am not leaving you here with that man!"

Momma was a woman of strong faith. She believed that even though the scars of war had permeated her family that healing was still available for her husband. "Deborah, bring me my Bible from the side-table in the dining room please."

Deb hesitated for a minute. The both of us had accompanied momma to church every Sunday of our entire lives and nothing had changed. The last thing Deb wanted to do at this point was to hear some Bible verses recited from the Bible.

"Deborah!" shouted Momma.

Deb reluctantly went into the dining room as instructed. During her absence, momma turned to me and said, "Son, the Bible teaches that we are to be like Jesus. Regardless of what happens around us, we are to be like Him in showing love. One day, you will have a family of your own. It is my prayer that you will not carry what you have seen and experienced in this house into your own house. Always remember that God is love and His love abides in you, me, Deborah and even your dad."

I stared into her loving and forgiving hazel eyes, trying desperately to understand what she was telling me. I hated my dad. Nothing about him or our house reminded me of God or felt loving.

"Deborah, will you please bring me my Bible like I asked," Momma shouted.

There was dead silence coming from the dining room. Deborah had completely disappeared. She knew our dad would be coming home soon so she took refuge in our parent's bedroom. Hiding deep inside the corner of the clothing closet was an old shoebox tucked away on the top shelf of the closet that held a 1958 Beretta 70 handgun. Although my dad rarely frequented the old shoebox, Deborah remembered it from her childhood.

She remembered him pulling out the handgun to clean it, oil it, load it, placing it back into the box and then hiding it deep into the corner of the closet. She also remembered the first time she saw him holding the gun as she peered into the bedroom from the hallway. Motioning for her to come closer, our dad waved the gun in her face:

"It's for protection. This is not a toy Deborah. Do you understand me?"

"Yes, daddy." Deb responded.

Deborah hadn't thought about the gun until momma insisted that she retrieve the Bible. In Deb's mind this would be the last time dad would hit momma or, God forbid, have sex with her. She took the gun and hid it in her clothing, ran down to the dining room, retrieved the Bible and headed back to the kitchen.

"What took you so long, Deborah?" momma asked. "Why didn't you answer when I called you?"

"I had to go to the bathroom," Deborah said. "Here's your Bible, momma."

Momma asked Deborah to turn to her favorite scripture in 1 Corinthians. Deborah handed the Bible back to momma and she began reading:

If I speak with the tongues of men and of angels, but do not have love, I have become a noisy gong or a clanging cymbal. If I have the gift of prophecy, and know all mysteries and all knowledge; and if I have all faith, so as to remove mountains, but do not have love, I am nothing. And if I give all my possessions to feed the poor, and if I surrender my body to be burned, but do not have love, it profits me nothing. And if I give all my possessions to feed the poor, and if I surrender my body to be burned, but do not have love, it profits me nothing. Love is patient, love is kind and is not jealous; love does not brag and is not arrogant; does not act unbecomingly; it does not seek its own, is not provoked, does not take into account a wrong suffered, or rude. Does not rejoice in unrighteousness, but rejoices with the truth; Bears all things, believes all things, hopes all things, endures all things. Love is patient, love is kind and is not jealous; love does not brag and is not arrogant, does not act unbecomingly; it does not seek its own, is not provoked, does not take into

*account a wrong suffered, does not rejoice in
unrighteousness, but rejoices with the truth; bears
all things, believes all things, hopes all things,
endures all things. Love never fails; but if there are
gifts of prophecy, they will be done away; if there
are tongues, they will cease; if there is knowledge,
it will be done away. For we know in part and we
prophesy in part; but when the perfect comes, the
partial will be done away. When I was a child, I
used to speak like a child, think like a child, reason
like a child; when I became a man, I did away with
childish things. For now we see in a mirror dimly,
but then face to face; now I know in part, but then I
will know fully just as I also have been fully known.
But now faith, hope, love, abide these three; but the
greatest of these is love.* [2]

Momma closed the Bible and stared at the two of us. I read this passage to the two of you to help increase your faith. You need to understand that the man your father has become is not the man I fell in love with, married or conceived two beautiful children with. Life has a funny way of portraying truth. Despite all the things we have gone through—through every adversity and challenge—I know your father still loves us and does not want to cause us harm. Deborah threw herself in the chair in defiance. I had never

---

[2] 1 Corinthians 13:1-13, NAS

seen my sister look so angry before and it frightened me. Momma reached out to grab Deborah's hand.

"Deborah, sweetheart, look at me? Deborah!" momma yelled, trying to snap her out of the trance she was in.

Love is never impatient but kind and void of judgment.

I need the two of you to understand that love is patient and kind. It is not jealous, does not brag nor is not arrogant. Love does not act unbecoming or seek its own. It is not easily provoked, does not consider all the wrongs suffered or rejoice in unrighteousness. It only rejoices in the truth. Love bears all things, believes all things, hopes in all things and endures all things. No matter how hard life has been, how you have been made to feel or what you have seen, I need the two of you to remember that love never fails. I could sense momma's heart and knew that she was trying to get us to understand the nature of forgiveness and how love influences the heart.

Deborah jumped to her feet and shouted out to momma. "I hear what you are saying momma but what he has done and continues to do is just not right! We need to leave momma and I mean right now!"

Before momma could respond, we heard the rattling of dad's keys trying to unlock the door. Everyone except Deborah froze. When dad entered the house, he was confronted by Deborah, who was holding his handgun and now pointing it at him. Before anyone could react three shots rang out and dad fell to the floor. One bullet hit dad in the leg, another in his shoulder and a third in his head. Momma jumped to her feet screaming. "Danny! Danny!" Momma grabbed dad's head while crying and rocking him in her bosom. In a state of shock, Deborah pulled the trigger again and inadvertently shot momma. There was a deafening silence in the air as the bodies of both of my parents lie dormant on the floor like a dirty pile of laundry.

"Deborah, what have you done?" I screamed.

I could not believe what was happening. Before I could say another word, Deb turned the gun on herself and pulled the trigger.

Falling to my knees I yelled out, "Deb, no! No!"

I was ten years old at the time. In that single moment, I felt the darkness of hatred invade my being. Momma had taken the time to teach us about love. In the blink of an eye, everything and everybody I loved was taken from me. Ever since that day, I have been at war fighting for my life.

WITHOUT A VOICE

"How do you enter the church and see three caskets laid before the congregation and worship God? If God was God how did he let this happen? He took my momma and my sister. Why not take that rotten man I called dad? Why did he take everybody I loved? I thought. Everyone at the church tried showing me compassion but it was bittersweet in my mouth. I kept thinking to myself, "God, you are such a hypocrite! Your stupid Bible says that we are to love. Who and what am I supposed to love! Your stupid Bible says we are to forgive. Well, I don't feel like forgiving and I will never forgive you!"

What proceeds from your mouth can determine your destiny, so guard it wisely.

Shortly after my declaration, I lost all ability to speak. All the psychologists I visited said it was due to shock. However, the real reason would reveal itself in time. Somehow, I had fallen into a war that I never asked for, sought after or intentionally chose to engage. It somehow landed in my lap, transforming me into a WAR BABY. I became shut off from the world—a world without family or speech—and found myself falling into a dark place. I remembered having this dream:

> I was home in the living room with my family. I had walked into the kitchen to get something from the fridge but when I turned around I couldn't get back to the living room. The kitchen floor had opened and I saw what appeared to be hell. Within it was a lake of fire. Everything was burning and I could feel the heat coming from it. The hole in the floor was not that big. I thought if I could just jump over it I could reach the other side. But when I did jump, the hole opened wider and half of my body was dangling inside the hole. Something was pulling me in as I gripped the sides of the hole. When I called out to momma, Deb and my dad for help, they just looked at me and did nothing. As it continued to pull me in, I could feel it cutting into my skin. It was hurting me so bad and it was getting unbearably hot. I began screaming frantically but no one would help me. I was barely hanging on with my right hand when a huge hand (like a man's hand) grabbed me. I never saw a face or body but I heard a voice. He said, "Not Daniel, he's mine! Now release him!" Suddenly, the hole in the kitchen floor that once tried to swallow me, ejected me and slowly began to close.

I woke up from that nightmare having no clue what it meant. The strangest thing is it was not the first time I had experienced the dream this intensely. Previously, I had only experienced bits and pieces of the dream but not enough to see the whole dream played out. Unbeknown to me, I would continue to have this dream over and over again.

By September 1990, I had been in and out of at least six foster homes. It was during my residency at the Wyandanch Foster Home that I met my best friend Zeke. The Wyandanch Foster Home housed at least thirty boys, ranging in ages five to seventeen years old. When I arrived, everyone welcomed me with open arms. I was about 6' 3" at the time and most of the guys thought I was at least eighteen years old or older but I was only fifteen years old. The Chancellor of the school must have mentioned that I did not talk and no one pressed me to do otherwise, except Zeke.

Zeke was seventeen years old at the time and a frequent runner. He was the second oldest of six children and made a point of always running away from home. His brother, Pete, owned the streets and Zeke got all his street smarts from him. The Chancellor felt sorry for Zeke and invited him to stay at the Wyandanch Foster Home as a matter of protection. Zeke and I became extremely tight and he quickly began teaching this ole 'church boy' how to survive in the real world. Zeke always had my back and I looked up to him. But little did I know my life was about to make a drastic shift.

It was in the early spring of March 1991 when Pastor Richard Therault and Mrs. Madeline Therault showed up at the door of the foster home. They seemed like a very nice couple. Some of the staff showed them around the facility, later escorting them into the Chancellor's office. It had been exactly five years, eight months and eleven days since the fatal shooting of my parents and sister Deborah, and I had never spoken a word since. I was watching the television sitcom, Death Wish, when the Superintendent of the home motioned for me to go with him to the Chancellor's office:

"Daniel, this is Pastor Richard and Mrs. Madeline Therault," the Chancellor stated.

They both looked at me and almost in unison said, *"Hello, Daniel!"* I looked at them, wanting to say something but nothing would come out of my mouth.

"Pastor and Mrs. Therault, I believe that if Daniel could have access to a loving environment, he would find his voice again," the Chancellor said.

That was pretty much the end of my introduction and interview with the Therault's. They exchanged pleasantries with the Chancellor and his staff and left the foster home; and I went back to watching my sitcom. Aware of the foster care process and the previous failed relationships with other foster parents, I was convinced that I was going to be a permanent resident of Wyandanch Foster Home, which was perfectly fine with me. To the contrary, on November 15,

1991, I received the best birthday present ever. Pastor Richard and Mrs. Madeline returned to the foster home and took me back with them to live in their home.

Pastor Richard and Mrs. Madeline ("Pastor Dick" and "Ms. Maddy") lived in Amityville, New York with their four children, Samson the dog and Mirage the cat. Pastor Dick was the Senior Pastor of Amityville Baptist Church for at least twelve years and was attuned to the Spirit of God. He constantly shared the story of how the Holy Spirit led him to the Wyandanch Foster Home, revealing that he would meet a fair-skinned redhead teenage boy with hazel eyes named Daniel; and how this little boy would become the son that he never had.

Pastor Dick and Ms. Maddy had four girls all ranging between four and twelve years old. They were hesitant to conceive another child, for fear of having another daughter. Pastor Dick would always joke from the pulpit: "Fathers, always subject yourself to the women of the house, no matter the age." He described it as a scripture verse hidden within the depths of the Bible.

In addition to pastoring, Pastor Dick worked at a local hardware store while Ms. Maddy was a stay at home wife. The Therault home was clean and quaint with few modern amenities. There was one television that broadcasted from the only three stations in the area, which was shared by everyone in the family. The home had access to dial-up internet only, which was never used by any of us children. To top it off, there were only three bedrooms, two bathrooms, a combined living/dining room and a small kitchen.

When I moved in, Chelsea (their oldest daughter) was forced to share a bedroom with her three other sisters—a move that did not set well with Chelsea to say the least. Nonetheless, living with the Therault family was an amazing experience. I became a big brother to Chelsea, age 12, Melissa, age 10, Courtney, age 8 and Maddy, age 4. Each one of the girls had their own unique personality, which I found amusing and quite adorable. Since Pastor Dick was the pastor of a church, it was expected that everyone in the home would attend church at least twice a week. I was not keen on going to church for obvious reasons but went anyway, purely out of respect for Ms. Maddy who reminded me of momma.

Once after Bible study, Pastor Dick treated us to ice-cream from the corner deli. It was a wonderful treat for me because Pastor Dick rarely could afford these types of splurges. After arriving home on one of those occasions, the seven of us stayed up to continue our discussion:

*"Now is my soul troubled; and what shall I say?
Father, save me from this hour. But for this cause
came I unto this hour. Father, glorify thy name.
There came therefore a voice out of heaven, saying,
I have both glorified it, and will glorify it again. The
multitude therefore, that stood by, and heard it, said
that it had thundered: others said, An angel hath
spoken to him. Jesus answered and said, This voice
hath not come for my sake, but for your sakes. Now
is the judgment of this world: now shall the prince
of this world be cast out. And I, if I be lifted up from
the earth, will draw all men unto myself."[3]*

"Pastor, I'm confused," Ms. Maddy said.

"Why are you confused, sweetheart?"

"If Jesus came to earth to take on the sins of the world, meaning that He died for our sins, then why would He say: 'Now my heart is troubled, and what shall I say? Father, save me from this hour?'"

"Yeah, daddy." Chelsea responded, "The whole point of Jesus coming to earth was to die, right?"

"Ok ladies, give a man a chance to answer," Pastor Dick chuckled.

First off, Jesus knew that the crucifixion was ahead of Him. But remember, He was not only spirit (Godly in nature) but also flesh (human in nature). The human side of Him

---

[3] John 12:27-32, NIV

dreaded the fate that lie before Him and yet He was submitted to the will of God. He knew that in taking on the sins of the world that it would require His sacrificial death, as well as His resurrection unto the Father. Now, before you ask, notice that Jesus declared as much when He made the statement, "But for this purpose I came to this hour." (v.27b). What most Believer's fail to notice is what took place after Jesus said, "Father, glorify Your name." (v. 28a):

"...Then a voice came out of heaven: "I have both glorified it, and will glorify it again. So the crowd of people who stood by and heard it were saying that it had thundered; others were saying, "An angel has spoken to Him."[4]

Most Believers pray and call on the name of the Lord all the time. And yet, we are convinced that God does not hear us or answer our prayers, when in truth He hears and answers our prayers all the time. So, the real question is why don't we hear him? (The family continues reading). Jesus answered and said:

"This voice has not come for My sake, but for your sakes. Now judgment is upon this world; now the ruler of this world will be cast out. And I, if I am lifted up from the earth, will draw all men to Myself."[5]

---

[4] John 12:28-29, NAS
[5] John 12:31-32, NAS

There was something in verses 30-32 that continued to resonate in my mind. I discreetly slipped a piece of paper to Pastor Dick with the question: What did Jesus mean when He said, "This voice has not come for My sake, but yours?" (v. 30).

"Family, Daniel wants to know what Jesus meant when He said, this voice has not come for my sake but for yours. Does anyone want to take a shot at answering his question?" Pastor Dick asked.

"You explained it earlier," said Chelsea.

"God speaks to His people all the time but for some reason we don't hear Him. So, if Jesus said this voice is not for Him but for us, then we need to listen to the Holy Spirit so we can hear from God; or at least that's what I think it means."

Pastor Dick looked at his wife, Maddy.

"She is amazing, isn't she? Just think, at such a tender age she can hear the voice of God in the clap of thunder!" gloated Pastor Dick.

"Daniel, do you have any further questions or comments to add?

"No, I'm just really tired. May I be excused?"

"Absolutely!" declared Pastor Dick.

"I need to put the girls to bed, honey," said Ms. Maddy.

Pastor Dick found himself sitting at the table alone. He loved having these types of Bible discussions between his family members and himself. I excused myself and went to bed. I remembered feeling extremely exhausted beyond usual. I climbed into bed with all the energy I could muster, remembering those last few words and how I was going to ask Pastor Dick about the passage: "Now judgment is upon this world; now the ruler of this world will be cast out. If I'm lifted up from the earth, will draw all men to myself." I slowly drifted off to sleep.

Sometime in the early hours of the next morning, I had the dream again but this time it was slightly different:

There was a lake of fire. Everything was burning and the heat coming from it was literally burning me. When I opened my eyes, I saw this dark image and it was laughing at me. It spoke to me and said, "You have nowhere to go unless I send you." I began to sense that *it* was not alone. There were hundreds of little dark things trying to get at me while I was in the bed. The bed was too high and as hard as they tried to reach me they could not. The room was becoming unbearably hot. Out of the corner of my eye, the things were building a bridge to get to me. I tried screaming but nothing came out. They were getting close to me. I could feel the heat coming from them and they had what appeared to be razor sharp-like teeth all over them. Just before they attempted to jump on the bed, I was awakened by a knock on the door.

"Son are you going to school today?" Pastor Dick said.

I quickly leaped out of bed and happy to be rid of that nightmare. Weekends seemed to end so quickly and here it was, Sunday again and time to go to church. The Amityville Baptist Church represented a small middle-class congregation that were of a mixed demographic, a rather close-knit fellowship. Pastor Dick allowed me to do handy jobs around the church, from changing light bulbs, unclogging drains, ensuring that the sanctuary was always ready for worship.

Pastor Dick was a great teacher of the Bible. He could take the most complex scriptures and make them easy to understand. Ms. Maddy, on the other hand, had a voice like an angel. She always sang just before her husband preached. My job was to keep the girls focused while in church, a task that was becoming increasingly challenging to say the least. Although Chelsea was twelve, she was very developed for her age and had raging hormones to complement her anatomy. Keeping an eye on her and Seth Schmidt was challenging. Seth was around sixteen or seventeen and played on the Amityville varsity football team. He and his two younger brothers always sat in a pew opposite to us. Their father was the Senior Deacon and his mother the organist and choir director of the church. Chelsea and Seth would constantly flirt with each other during the service.

A fidgety person by nature, Seth was in and out of the church smoking a cigarette. One Sunday, I happened to notice that both Chelsea and Seth were missing. Leaving Melissa in charge, I set out to look for the two of them. As I approached the back-office downstairs I could hear noises coming from behind the door and when I opened the door, there they were. I immediately reached in to grab Chelsea but before I knew it Seth had punched me in the face. The blow hit me so hard that I fell to the floor. He angrily dared me to say anything to Pastor Dick or Ms. Maddy. As I lay on the floor with a bloody nose, Chelsea just smirked at me and walked off with Seth. Regaining my composure, I went back into the sanctuary where I found Chelsea and Seth pretending as if nothing had happened. I wanted to tell Pastor Dick about Chelsea and everything that had happened but I did not know how to express it since I still could not speak.

Pastor Dick and Ms. Maddy's home had a warm and calming aura. Ms. Maddy was a homemaker and she always had a hot meal ready and waiting for the family. The table looked like a feast prepared for a king. I never could understand how she could create such a spread but there was always fresh baked cornbread, rice and beans and some sort of meat on the table with each setting. As a family, we would hold hands and say grace to bless the food and afterwards exchange stories about the happenings of that day. One evening, through an exchange of notes, Pastor Dick asked me to share something about my day. I wrote down how Pastor Dick had coached me through so many situations. Chelsea immediately chimed in saying, "What are you asking him for? Ain't he retarded? Isn't that why he can't speak?" I slammed my fork in my plate, jumped up from the table and went to my room. Ms. Maddy, called out, "Daniel!"

As I stomped off to my room, I could hear Ms. Maddy chastising her daughter and demanding that she apologize.

"What for?" Chelsea screamed, "He's so dumb! He doesn't talk and he acts like a girl!"

Pastor Dick shouted, "Ok, that's enough Chelsea! Go to your room!"

The other three girls just sat in silence. Pastor Dick later came to my room. He knocked and entered as was customary.

"Daniel, may I come in?" he said.

I looked at him, wanting to share everything I knew about Chelsea but no words would come out of my mouth.

"Daniel, I know that you have been through a terrible ordeal. I can't imagine how you must feel but know that love is always patient and kind."

Before he could continue, I screamed at the top of my voice:

"Love is not patient or kind! Momma read that scripture and then she, my dad and my sister all died! I hate you! I hate you, the church, Chelsea and my life! Now leave me alone get out of my room!" I yelled.

Shocked that I had finally spoken, Pastor Dick stood frozen in place. Ms. Maddy and the girls ran into the room, equally shocked that I had spoken but more mortified by what I had said and how I had spoken to Pastor Dick. I knew then that I had to leave their home. So, while everyone was asleep that night, I gathered my belongings and I left.

THE GOOD LIFE

When I left Amityville, I had nowhere to go. The only familiar place I knew was the Wyandanch Foster Home and that is exactly where I headed. For the next four years, I stayed in the foster home at night while trying to find some form of employment by day. The foster home seemed strangely unfamiliar and different from when I last stayed there; and trying to secure an honest job seemed almost impossible. While walking home one evening, I ran across my old buddy Zeke. He was sporting a Versace suit and wearing Gucci shoes. Seeing me in the distance he yelled out:

"Danny is that you? Wow, look at you!"

"No man, look at you!"

Zeke appeared stunned as if not comprehending how or why I was talking. After all, the last time we saw each other I was not talking at all.

"So, he speaks finally! So, what are you up to man?"

"Man, I'm trying to find a job!"

"Man, I got the perfect job for you! I'm working with this investment firm."

"Investments? I don't know anything about investing."

"Man, you don't need to know nothin'. Look man it's easy. I move the product and my broker ensures that I get paid. It's that simple."

"I'll have to think about it, Zeke."

"Well, don't think too long. I don't know how long they'll be recruiting!"

Zeke had left the foster home about a year prior to me leaving the Therault's home. His brother Pete was the main broker or investor for Wyandanch. I had never done investing but if it could get me somewhere safe to live and food in my mouth, then I was all in. I went back to the foster home and met with the Chancellor to tell him about my encounter with Zeke. He agreed that I should consider getting involved as the organization was always looking for great talent. Little did I know the Chancellor was a corrupt dealer and using the foster home as a front for his illegal actions.

That night I had the first peaceful rest and decided to find Zeke in the morning. I noticed Zeke sitting in Liza's Deli having breakfast. The deli was the only decent eatery on Main Street. Zeke saw me and invited me to join him for breakfast. Staring at Zeke from across the table, I was thinking: "Boy, Zeke's features have changed a lot. He looked bad and gaunt."

"So, man, how you really doing? You look awfully thin." I asked.

"Man, I'm good. Just need to get a good shot of apple juice and I'll be on point!"

"Apple juice does that for you? Well, ok, then I'll have some too!" I said jokingly.

Zeke lunged across the table so quickly that it literally scared me. He was dead serious and not joking around with me.

"Man, if I ever hear of you touching any apple juice, I will beat you silly!"

"Ok, ok!" I replied. "All I'm trying to say is that I'm ready to start working with you."

We embraced with a brotherly hug and I never brought up the subject of apple juice again.

"Look man, I'm really glad we're going to be working the same business together but we got to work on your image! The clients we service need us to look good all the time." Zeke stated.

"So, what's wrong with my clothes?"

"Man, you look like you should be in a choir or something. You've got to pack up that church look or you'll scare the customers."

"Well then hook a brotha up!" I mocked.

Zeke and I shook hands and he gave me an advance of $10,000. I had never seen so much money before. Afterwards, I purchased some choice pieces of clothing, secured a used Audi S4 convertible and an apartment, all for about five and a half grand. I placed the balance in a bank account. The jobs I was given were easy. Go to point A, pick up a package and bring it to Zeke. Everyone seemed authentic and I had no reservations about the work. Within a short period of time, I was easily raking in about 10-15% off the top of every delivery, once the payout was received. After three years of working this gig, I found myself bringing in at least seven thousand dollars every run. I am twenty-four years old and my life had made a complete 360° turn around. I had money, I owned my own townhouse and I had plenty of women. Sometimes, I would wake up and there would be at least two or three beautiful women in the bed with me. Life was good!

––––––––––––

Be careful what and how you define as a good life, for it may be laced with evil.

––––––––––––

It was around 10:00 am when the phone rings. It was Zeke.

"Hey, man what's up? Look we got to meet with the main broker around 12:00 pm today." Zeke responded.

"Come on man! Today? Today is not a good day cause I got company." I stated.

"Listen, you got from now 'til about 11:30 am to do your company and meet me on Main at 12:00 and Danny I'm not joking!" Zeke said.

"Ok man, I'll be there. Why you sounding so intense?"

Zeke never responded but just hung up. As agreed, I arrived at 12:00 pm sharp at the corner of 12th and Main. Zeke was on the phone, pacing up and down the sidewalk. I tooted my horn and he jumped in the car:

"So which way are we headed?" I asked.

"Westside, Amityville. You got your piece, right?" Zeke asked.

"Never leave home without it! Man, what's going on? Why you sweating so?" I asked.

Zeke did not respond. We drove in silence for the next twenty minutes.

"Zeke, what's going on?" I asked again.

"Ok Danny, I should've come clean some time ago!"

"Clean? Clean about what!" I said.

"This ain't funny, Danny!"

"So why are we meeting the main broker and why are you acting all nervous?"

"Danny, I'm sorry. I know I brought you in to be part of the team but, well ah, look I've been trying to kick my habit but it ain't working and I owe the man big time!" Zeke explained.

"Habit? What habit and what the hell does that have to do with me? I collect and bring the packages to you and you pay me from the clients!"

By now, I'm yelling at the top of my voice as I pull the car over to the layby.

"Man, what are you telling, me?" I shouted.

"Danny, you're cool. I'll take the hit and explain everything. We just need to go now or else we will be late!"

**Do not be blinded by deception.
It corrupts the soul.**

We were less than fifteen minutes away. I remember looking up towards heaven and quietly praying, "Oh God, please get me out of this!" As I drove in the back entrance of the stadium, there were four black Ford Explorers and they seemed to block the entrance once we entered. Within minutes, a black limo pulled up and the back door opened. The driver beckoned Zeke and I to come forward. As we got close to the vehicle I was startled. The Chancellor of my former foster home was getting out of the back of the vehicle.

"Chancellor?" I said.

He put his hand up as if to signal me to stop talking.

"What in the world are you doing here?" I asked him but he never answered.

His driver beckoned Zeke closer to the vehicle. They exchanged some words and within seconds I heard a single gunshot. The Chancellor shot Zeke at point blank range.

"What the hell!" I shouted.

Then the Chancellor pointed his gun at me:

"Look, I don't know what's going on, why I'm here or what you want with me! All I know is I discussed this gig with you and you said it was a great opportunity! So, why are you pointing a gun at me, Chancellor?" I shouted.

"I want you to know that if you ever think of doing what Zeke did to me, you will end up like him!" said the Chancellor.

He recoiled his weapon and got in the car. All the cars left the scene. It was just me and Zeke. I ran over to Zeke. I got this sharp pain in my chest. I was stunted for a quick second.

I remember crying out, "Oh, God, Zeke! Man, what have you done?"

When I turned him over, I felt a faint pulse. Zeke grabbed me by my shirt and with his last breath said, "Danny, get out!"

Those were the last words spoken by Zeke before he died.

A DARK ROAD

Later that day, I found myself driving around in circles, asking myself what I had gotten myself into. I had longed for success only to discover that life is shrouded by lies, secrets and deceit. I looked for success and now my life is wrapped up in this closed book. How do I get out of it? The job kept me busy but I had no clue whom to trust. So, I carried out my tasks trying to keep a low profile with the only friend I could trust—my Kahr PM handgun.

____

War: It provides a testing ground for your soul. Therefore, aim to always pass your test.

____

It was a cool Fall evening. I had worked hard and was out on the south side of Main Street looking for (let us say) some comfort. There were a few ladies and one, in particular, caught my eye. I have been on the stretch and knew all the ladies but this one was new to me. I pulled over; she looked uncannily familiar, very fair with these memorable blue eyes. As she leaned in the window of my car, she blurted out:

"I'll give you fifteen minutes for fifty bucks!"

"No, I'm good." I said.

I did not do drugs but it was clear that the girl was on something. I drove off but something in the back of my mind could not let it go. Something about the girl did not seem right. I could not pin point it but there was a "sound in the clap of thunder," that told me to go back. I swung the car around and just as I got to her, she was getting in Damon's car. Damon was a ruthless pimp. When his girls did not perform their bodies would end up in a dumpster. He normally kept his girls well drugged. As he and the girl drove off, I shouted, "Chelsea!" She looked back but her eyes went right through me.

"Oh God, not Chelsea," I thought.

I followed Damon's car to Sixth Street, ending up in front of apartment sixty-six. I jumped out of the car and confronted Damon with my piece loaded.

"Damon, let go of her!" I shouted.

"Man, please she's just trash and she owes me big time!"

"How much does she owe you? I'll pay whatever it is!"

"She's owes me about two grand!" Damon shouted.

Pulley, one of Damon's boys, shouted, "Day, everything ok?" Suddenly, there was a pap like sound and all hell broke loose. "Pap, pap, pap!" I took out Pulley and Damon as I watched Chelsea collapse from being shot. I rushed and grabbed Chelsea, racing her to Amityville Hospital, where I knew she would be safe. She was shot in the arm and only had a superficial wound. By the time we reached Amityville, I noticed that I had been shot too and was bleeding profusely. I remembered pushing on my chest because the pain was so intense. I got Chelsea admitted and gave them her name and contact details before collapsing on the floor in the emergency room. When I had awakened, I saw Pastor Dick sitting at the foot of my bed.

"Son, I'm so happy you are alive," he said.

His eyes welled up with tears and he had this genuine look of compassion for me, like a father for a son.

"Daniel, you were in ICU for a week. They just moved you yesterday to this ward. Son, you almost died."

As he spoke, tears were streaming down his cheeks. Until that moment, I never thought of Pastor Dick as a kind compassionate kind of guy. Pastor Dick was a six-foot, stocky built guy with reddish hair and a few freckles. We looked so much alike that a person could easily mistake me for being his natural born son. He had fair milky white skin and when he became flustered, his cheeks looked like double-layered marshmallows blushed with strawberries. I had not thought about that in a long time; and it made me think of momma and how she would often describe my cheeks that way. Pastor Dick was the dad that I never had.

"Hey, Pastor Dick, I was just thinking."

"Thinking about what?" he said.

"You remember when I was living with you guys, you used to brag about playing football in college? And how you would always say: 'Don't get confused by this physique! It used to be a well-defined six-pack but over time it settled, right here in my mid-section to a one-pack?' Well, I was just thinking how that one-pack is starting to overdevelop, so what's going on? You remember how Ms. Maddy would just shake her head every time you talked about it, as if she was disgusted by the mere mention of it?"

Pastor Dick laughed out loud. I muscled up a chuckle, trying not to laugh, due to all the pain I was in. For a brief second, Pastor Dick thought about Ms. Maddy. How he missed her. The atmosphere in the room became solemn and the pain from the surgery was becoming more severe.

"Pastor Dick, can you call the nurse for me? I think I need some meds for the pain. I just want to thank you for everything you have done for me. I'm so sorry I didn't turn out to be the ideal son that you and Ms. Maddy deserved. By the way, how is Chelsea?"

"She's in rehab now," Pastor Dick explained.

"What happened to her? How did she get so far off track?"

"Chelsea developed a dark streak," Pastor Dick said. "And became so rebellious and disrespectful that she began running away from home. Things got so bad with Chelsea that we frequently rallied together to search for her. Sometimes we would rally together and find her but then she would run off again. The last time she ran off we searched for her but could not find her."

"Pastor Dick, you always reminded me of the story of Jesus telling the people who had followed him about his true purpose and the impact it would have on them. I never forgot the sermon you preached, *Don't Miss the Sound in the Clap of the Thunder 'Cause It's For You*," I said with great authority.

"See Daniel, I told you there was a preacher in you somewhere!" We both laughed.

"No sir that ain't happening, Pastor Dick!"

"In all seriousness, Daniel, I've been sitting here trying to decipher what I would say to you when you woke up," said Pastor Dick. "The Holy Spirit led me to a particular passage in the Bible. May I read it to you?"

I nodded my head in affirmation as he started reading from a passage in the twelfth chapter of John:

*Now my soul is troubled, and what shall I say?
'Father, save me from this hour'? No, it was for this
very reason I came to this hour. Father, glorify your*

name!" Then a voice came from heaven, "I have glorified it, and will glorify it again. The crowd that was there and heard it said it had thundered; others said an angel had spoken to him. Jesus said, "This voice was for your benefit, not mine. Now is the time for judgment on this world; now the prince of this world will be driven out. And I, when I am lifted up from the earth, will draw all people to myself. He said this to show the kind of death he was going to die. The crowd spoke up, "We have heard from the Law that the Messiah will remain forever, so how can you say, 'The Son of Man must be lifted up'? Who is this 'Son of Man'?" Then Jesus told them, "You are going to have the light just a little while longer. Walk while you have the light, before darkness overtakes you. Whoever walks in the dark does not know where they are going. Believe in the light while you have the light, so that you may become children of light." When he had finished speaking, Jesus left and hid himself from them.[6]

As Pastor Dick closed the Bible, he looked at me with such fatherly love.

"Daniel, you must walk in the light before the darkness completely overtakes you. My son, you have an inept ability to hear the voice of God. It was His voice that redirected you to turn back to find our Chelsea. I know you want out. Just allow yourself to truly believe in the Light while He is still present. Daniel, the Lord is waiting on you to open the doors

---

[6] John 12:27-36, NIV

of your heart. You may have chosen a dark path but you do not have to stay on it. You can choose a better path but you must exercise faith. Trust that God is sovereign and able to do anything for you. Son, first you must believe that He can and will do it for you."

**Whatever the situation may demand,
exercise your faith.
Trust that God is sovereign.**

I could hear momma's words reverberating in my mind as Pastor Dick spoke. It had been a long time since I recalled her voice. Despite all the hurt that I had carried within me, her words rang true: "Love is not provoked" and it "does not take into account a wrong suffered." [7] Pastor Dick exemplified the love that momma used to talk about.

"Son, you look tired. I'll come back to see you another time," Pastor Dick said.

"How is Ms. Maddy?" I asked.

Pastor Dick rested his hand on my forehead, gently caressing my brow. "Get some rest, Daniel."

Pastor Dick remained briefly staring at me as I slowly drifted off to sleep. Unknown to me, here was a man who

---

[7] 1 Cor. 13:5, NAS

was riddled with a level of pain and grief that had escaped me. His daughter was being restored back to him and the beloved son that he thought he had lost had now returned. As joyous as the occasion was, it only partially quenched the pain of him losing his beloved wife at the hands of a drunk-driver. His heart was heavy and he knew at some point he would have to tell Daniel the truth.

"One step at a time," He mumbled to himself, "one step at a time."

EXTENDED FAMILY

As I laid in the hospital, I felt as though I was not alone. Whatever was in the room, its presence was dark and then it spoke.

It said to me, "I have power over you and you will only go, except when I send you."

I asked *it*, "What do you want from me?"

It replied, "I am the unholy trinity. Those who think they know me refer to me as the Antichrist but I am not. I am your savior. I have provided you with everything you have—riches, fame and even life. I am the beast who has control over you, Chelsea, Pastor Dick and all whom you call friend. I have made you my war baby so now you belong to me."

Somehow, the scripture Pastor Dick read to me the night before came back to me. In defiance, I spoke to the presence in the room:

"Jesus Christ the Light is here and no darkness shall prevail against me or overtake me!"

The dark presence screamed, "Ahhhh! I will come back for you!"

And just like that it left the room and I slowly drifted off to sleep, determined to get well and get out of the hospital. I was awakened yet again and there were three men in black standing over my bed.

"You're Danny Schmartz, right?" the bald guy asked.

"It depends on who is asking," I replied.

Appearing to be the spokesman of the group, he said, "I talk and you listen, or I'll put a cap in you right here in this hospital bed."

"Look man, what do you want?" I asked, trying to sit up in the bed.

"The Chancellor needs you to pick up a package for him and he says you are the only one who can do it!"

"Yeah, you guys are funny! You tell the Chancellor that I'm confined to bed and won't be able to make that appointment."

"Chancellor said you would probably say that. You familiar with a Chelsea Therault, right?"

"Who? Look, you leave her out of this!" I shouted.

"Too late. I believe her dad is the pastor of the Baptist Amityville Church. We already popped his wife a couple of months ago!"

The bald man looked back at the other two men and they all started laughing.

"Yep, the pastor's wife got hit by a drunk-driver."

"What the hell are you talking about? Ms. Maddy? What are you saying? She's dead?"

The room started spinning and I suddenly could not breathe. The man reached over and grabbed my oxygen mask, preventing me from getting any oxygen.

"The Chancellor expects you back at Wyandanch by Monday morning or the church is next!" he shouted, as they all left laughing.

Gasping for air, all I could think about is Ms. Maddy. The thought of her being dead consumed my heart with the same darkness that filled my room earlier.

"Oh God, not Ms. Maddy!" I yelled. "They are messing with the wrong person! I'm going to kill that bastard Chancellor if it's the last thing I do!"

"Nurse! Nurse!" I yelled.

Standing in the doorway, the nurse said, "Yes, Mr. Schmartz."

"I want a doctor!" I yelled. I need to be discharged and I'm leaving with or without the doctor's permission!"

"Mr. Schmartz, you are a very sick man. It is not in your best interest for us to discharge you right now." she responded calmly.

"Either help me or get out of my way!" I shouted.

The nurse left the room to summon help from one of the orderlies. By the time she returned, I was nowhere to be found. I stumbled out to the parking lot where my rental car was located. I knew something was not quite right about me but rage had overtaken my senses. I was on a mission and the only thing I could think of was, "I'm going to get that bastard Chancellor if it's the last thing I do!"

After being in business for a while, I had made some contacts. Zeke's brother, Pete, although retired still had his hand on the pulse of Wyandanch. There was no secret that the Chancellor was trying to cut into the market share. The fact that he killed Zeke was the ammunition I needed to recruit Pete. Chancellor walked a very thin line.

So, my first stop was to check in with Pete. Pete and Zeke's family lived near the Westside Wyandanch Foster Home. Peter ("Pete") Timbarlow, now in his early thirties, was about 5' 8" with a muscular build and the warmest smile ever. His picture-perfect smile had wooed many women off their feet but that was not always the case for Pete. The first time I met Pete, I was living at the foster home. He would always check on Zeke to make sure he was doing ok. I remember him always meeting with the Chancellor handing him an envelope, which I always assumed was to ensure that Zeke was well taken care of. For many years, I thought he was Zeke's dad by the way he interacted with Zeke and the Chancellor.

One day, Pete shared his story with me. I never understood why. Maybe it had something to do with him feeling safe around me because I did not talk. He talked for hours. Although his story was interesting, I was just a fifteen-year-old kid who had just been through the worst nightmare of his life. All I really wanted to do is watch my television show Death Wish. Nevertheless, I sat quietly giving Pete my undivided attention:

"Hey?" Pete said.

I just stared at him as he sat down to share his story:

"You know, things have been pretty tough for the Timbarlow family. Jimmy went to the store one day and never came back. With me being the oldest, I had to step up and be the man of the house to care for the family. I was only thirteen when Sylvie sent Jimmy to the store for some bread, milk and a quarter pound of ham. We never got the food and we never laid eyes on Jimmy ever again."

"Who's Sylvie and Jimmy?" I wrote on a piece of paper.

"My folks." Pete replied.

I wrote, "You called your parents by their first name?"

"Hell yeah!" Pete said.

I sat and looked at him, wondering what would have happened to me if I called my dad Daniel. I grimaced at the sheer thought of it, realizing I would probably be six feet under if I had done something like that. Pete continued with his story:

"Jimmy left Sylvie with six babies and never returned. About three years after that (I was around sixteen by then) I became the sole provider of the Timbarlow family. I had no time for school so I dropped out. The odd jobs I had was not enough to cover the needs of the family, so I was introduced to the business. Initially, I just worked for the Chancellor but quickly learned how evil and corrupt he was in his business dealings. Because I was a young pup and wet behind the ears, the Chancellor took advantage of me and that is when I met Red Cap. Well, Red Cap is the name everyone in the neighborhood called him but I just called him Red. Everyone got their start with Red and the Chancellor was no different. What I found interesting about Red is that he was originally a homeless kid. As soon as he saved up enough money, he started the Wyandanch Foster Home and appointed the Chancellor to run it. Within two years or so, the Chancellor had played Red so badly that he had acquired the loyalty of at least half of Red's security detail. Hoping to keep things on friendly terms, Red released the Chancellor and I stayed on with Red. Red treated me like a son. In return, the Timbarlow family was never in need of anything because of

Red. He was a good man who taught me everything I needed to know about the business and life in general." Pete said.

"So, Daniel, when you see me visiting the Chancellor it is because he made my brother Zeke a runner. Zeke was a man-pleaser and would do anything to gain attention. He ain't like me, man. In this business you got to be tough enough to make hard decisions. I honestly don't know why the Chancellor was the way he was. But what I do know is that I did not like how he used my brother, knowing full well he was just a kid. Hey man you hearing me, right?" asked Pete.

Before I could respond to Pete, he started up his story again.

"I couldn't believe the Chancellor would stoop so low as to recruit my brother into his nasty rink, while he was still living at the foster home. Secondly, the Chancellor knew Zeke was weak and wet behind the ears. Chancellor would always put him in dangerous situations, sending him to collect packages from the worst connections in Long Island like Shorty. Hey, don't let the name Shorty fool you. I remember one night I followed Zeke to make sure that he was safe. Zeke was still a kid and one of Shorty's guys saw me in the distance. Man, they beat me up pretty bad. They broke two of my ribs and knocked out two of my back teeth.

I was determined after that, just because I was skinny, ain't nobody going to beat me up again. So, I went to Red and he hooked me up with Doc Schneider, the best boxer to ever come out of the Westside. I trained with him for about a year and that's how I got this physique."

Pete started flexing his muscles. I might have been big and tall but my muscles were nothing like Pete's. His muscle was the size of my thigh. I chucked to myself thinking about taking one of my thighs and putting it on my arm. Pete noticed I was losing focus:

"You're still with me, right?"

I nodded my head "yes" as Pete continued.

"The Chancellor complained that Zeke owed him a great deal of money. But if the real story be told, Zeke wanted out and wanted to leave with me to go back home. But the Chancellor kept making it harder and harder for him to leave. So, Zeke thought if he ran away from the shelter, he could get away from the Chancellor."

———

The long drive to Wyandanch had allowed for a time of reflection but I needed to refocus. I was enraged over Ms. Maddy's death that I never stopped to think about my own health. The pain in my abdomen was intensifying. My rash behavior and departure from the hospital in Amityville had put my health in jeopardy. Unknown to me, the doctors never got a chance to tell me that a live bullet was still lodged in my abdomen. Now, that bullet was traveling through my body and causing me a great deal of pain.

I finally arrived in Wyandanch on Sunday evening, just before dusk. Since no one expected me until the following day, I arrived under the radar unnoticed. I had already called ahead and talked to Pete, advising him of what time to expect me. The townhouse and area where he lived was highly guarded. As I approached in my rental car, everyone was packing some major heat and ready to unload. Pete came running out to flag me down and invite me into his home:

"Man, you look like hell!" Pete said.

"Man, I feel like hell."

I had already briefed Pete on my hospital encounter with the Chancellor's goonies.

"So, Pete, what's the plan?" I asked.

"Listen, Danny, we need to do everything as planned with the Chancellor. When we can catch him off guard then we can make our move. That's the best way to take him down." said Pete.

"No, I think we should show up at the foster home and put a cap in him!"

"Man, after all the stuff you went through with your family being shot up and stuff, you'd be willing to risk those kids seeing that?" asked Pete.

Pete's response was the slap in the face that I needed.

"Look Pete, don't forget that bastard took out Zeke and Ms. Maddy. I don't see any need for any respect."

"What do you mean that he took out Zeke?"

Pete froze in place waiting on a response from me.

"Look Pete, about a month ago Zeke asked me to take him to the Eastside location and he was telling me that he was in debt because he drank too much apple juice."

"Apple juice!" Pete said. "My brother wasn't on drugs! That no good Chancellor!"

"Yeah, I know. But Zeke was in Liza's place when he told me that he was waiting on some apple juice."

Pete looked at me and stared. "Ok, church boy, so what else happened?"

"Church boy? I haven't been to church in years." I thought. "Wonder why he is calling me a church boy?"

Refocusing, I continued with my story:

"So, we met at this stadium and the Chancellor came out of this black limousine. He called Zeke up to the car and the next thing I heard was "bam!" Chancellor had shot Zeke at point blank range."

I could see a fiery rage stirring inside of Pete as he paused to try and gain his composure.

"Ok, Danny, I hear you but we still need to plan this thing out. We don't need any extra casualties, so either we do it my way or you're on your own." Pete said.

"Ok, Pete. I'm not feeling that good anyway and my wound is beginning to bleed again! You got some place where I can lay my head? I need somewhere to lay my head?"

"Chump, take Danny to Zeke's old room so he can rest! Charlotte, can you pop to the pharmacy? We're going to need some pain meds and sterile dressing!" Pete shouted, barking orders to his crew.

I made my way upstairs and finally climbed into the bed, wondering what in the world was wrong with me. I had never felt such excruciating pain in my life! After Charlotte returned from the pharmacy, she cleaned and redressed my wound, gave me a couple pain pills and that was the last thing I remembered.

Meanwhile, Pete was reflecting on everything I had told him. He rallied his men together and told them that the drop on the Chancellor had to happen that night. Pete was well connected and had been in the business for more than twenty years. He had established just as many contacts as the

Chancellor. After sending a couple of informants, the word came back that the Chancellor would be out and about making visits on the Eastside of Wyandanch. Pete made a couple of calls to some of his Eastside connections:

"Hey, this is Pete. The Chancellor and his gang are coming to your side of town for a pick up."

"What's up man?" the responder asked.

"I just found out it was the Chancellor who put a cap in my little brother, Zeke." Pete replied.

"Chancellor from Westside?" asked the responder.

"Yep, that's the one. He and his entourage are not to leave alive once he enters your side."

"Consider it done." the responder said.

The hit took place on Monday morning around 1:45 a.m. It was the worst blood bath ever on the Eastside. The Chancellor and his gang rode into an ambush and no one survived. Unknown to Pete, one of his guys (Kevin aka "Sleezie") also worked for the Chancellor. Sleezie kept tabs on Pete, informing the Chancellor on whatever plans Pete had and vice-versa. On the night of the hit, Sleezie had already leaked the hit to Chancellor, which meant that the Chancellor managed to escape with his life in tack.

In retaliation, the Chancellor setup a sting on Pastor Dick's entire church and his daughter, Chelsea. Later that evening (or sometime in the early hours of the next morning), I had the dream again but this time it made more sense:

> I was at home in the living room with my family. On this occasion my family was Pastor Dick and Ms. Maddy. I walked into the kitchen to get something from the fridge but when I turned around I could not get back to the living room. The kitchen floor had opened and I saw hell (or what appeared to be hell) with a lake of fire within it. Everything was burning and the heat coming from it was literally burning me. Since the hole was not that big, I thought if I could just jump over it that I could reach the other side. When I did jump, the hole opened wider until half of my body was dangling inside the hole. Something was pulling me in and when I called out to Pastor Dick and Ms. Maddy for help, they both just looked at me and did nothing. As it continued to try and pull me in, I could feel it cutting into my skin. It was hurting me so bad and it was getting unbearably hot. I began to scream frantically but no one would help me. I was barely hanging on with my right hand when a huge hand (like a man's hand) grabbed me. I never saw a face or body but I heard a voice. He said, 'Not Daniel, he's mine. Now release him.' Suddenly, the hole in the kitchen floor that once tried to swallow me, ejected me and slowly began to close.

After a good night's rest, I came downstairs to find Pete smoking a jay and looking really relaxed.

"I'm getting ready to head out, Pete." I said.

"Man, no need. It's done."

"What's done?" I asked.

Before he could answer, Charlotte came running into the room screaming: "Turn on the news! Turn on the news!"

Charlotte turned on the television and I could not believe what I was hearing or seeing. Amityville Baptist Church was on fire!

"What day is this?" I screamed.

"It's Wednesday!" Charlotte shouted.

I was frantic, "When did this happen?"

"Sometime last night!" Charlotte said.

"Oh God! Tuesday is Bible study night! Oh God! Oh God! I gotta go!"

"Danny, you ain't fit to go anywhere! Sit." Pete said.

"Chump, take a few of the guys and head over to the church and get us a report!" Pete ordered.

"On it!" Chump said.

Chump and a group of Pete's men rushed out the door. Not long after, a newscaster reported that prior to the church catching on fire, it appeared that someone had opened fire and shot everyone in the church. It was assumed that the Pastor was inside the church but nothing could be confirmed until the fire was brought under control. Charlotte headed towards the kitchen and overheard some whispering from the corner of the back porch:

"Yeah boss. Pete just sent over a few guys. Yeah, yeah, they fell for it. No, Danny is not in the bunch. Still here at the house," Sleezie said.

Stunned by what she heard, Charlotte attempted to run out of the kitchen, inadvertently knocking over a pan on the stove in the process. Noticing her, Sleezie pulled out his silencer to shoot, lunging at her to put his hand over her mouth as he shot her in the side. Before running out the back door, he dragged her lifeless body and threw her into the linen closet. Meanwhile, Pete and I were still in the living room talking about the hit that had happened the night before.

"Man, tell me what you did again?" I asked.

"Listen Danny, you don't need any additional blood on your hands. I'm well connected and it's done!" Pete said.

Trying to convince Pete that I was well enough to go, Pete ignored me and started calling out for Charlotte.

**War is without prejudice.
Its mark can leave long-lasting scars.**

"Charlie? Charlotte girl, where you at?" Pete yells. "That girl is always on a mission. She's a fighter and I love her. You know, Danny, she's been with me since the beginning of time."

Charlotte was critically injured but still alive! The fall to the floor had knocked her out and she was bleeding profusely. Being the fighter that she was, Charlotte stumbled into the living room collapsing on the floor.

Pete jumped up and screamed. "Charlie!" he yelled.

Charlotte's blood was everywhere.

"I love you, Pete," she whispered and with her last breath she mouthed, "Sleezie."

Pete cradled her bloody body while yelling and crying obscenities. In a few seconds, she was gone.

The only thing I could think to say is, "Pete, man, I'm so sorry." But I knew my heartfelt condolences could never fill the void of what Pete was feeling over the loss of his beloved Charlotte.

Pete looked up at me and in between his agonizing groans yelled, "Charlotte! My dear sweet Charlie! What am I going to do without my Charlie?"

With Chump and crew gone to Amityville, Pete's security detail was rather slim. There was a clap of thunder saying, "Check the surveillance and run it backwards."

"Pete ain't you got some surveillance here at the house?" I said.

"Pete, listen to me!" I shouted. "Do you have some video surveillance or something around here?"

"Yeah, take my phone," Pete said, pointing to his phone on the table.

I began reviewing the video surveillance footage on Pete's phone from current time, moving backwards.

"Pete, you have got to see this!" I said.

Pete gently rested Charlotte's head on the floor and came over to me. The surveillance clearly showed that Sleezie had shot Charlotte but it also captured Sleezie's conversation.

"How many men you have here for security detail?" I asked.

"Not many. Maybe five or six." Pete responded.

"Man, it ain't enough. Can you make a phone call?" I said.

"Yeah, but my connections are over on the Eastside. It'll take them about twenty to thirty minutes to get over here."

"Pete, you have to make the call! I have a hunch that it's going to be a blood bath!"

"Pete, where's your stash!" I yelled again.

"Look man, I'm not trying to be insensitive but Charlie is gone! The Chancellor's probably on his way here. Pete, snap out of it!"

Pete finally called the remainder of his security detail to give them a heads up on what was about to go down.

"I need you to reach out to Chump and the gang too!" he ordered.

"Danny my stash is in the linen closet." Pete shouted.

I went to the closet and all I saw was linen. Pete, following behind me, lifting a fake light cover to reveal a hidden room. The room must have been the length of the whole house with enough firepower to take out an entire army.

Pete, looked at me and said, "Let's go, war baby!"

The war I tried so hard to avoid finally caught up with me. Here I am in the midst of an intrinsic inflammatory position for acquisition—an acquisition defined by my life and the lives of all those I now call family.

FINDING REFUGE

As Chump and the guys rolled up to the Amityville Baptist Church, the stench of burnt flesh was rancid. The police and fire department where still on the scene. Chump did his own investigative work only to find out that neither the Pastor nor his children had attended Bible study that evening. Pastor Dick had received an emergency call from the rehabilitation center where Chelsea was residing. His remaining daughters—Melissa (13), Courtney (11) and Maddy (7) insisted on traveling with their dad to see Chelsea.

When Pastor Dick and the girls heard the news about the church burning and shooting, they headed back as quickly as they could to the scene. Upon his arrival, Pastor Dick spoke with the police, confirming that Deacon Schmidt as one of many listed as dead. Deacon Schmidt had requested to facilitate the Bible study that evening and, beyond that, Pastor Dick could not verify the names of anyone else in attendance. Chump was watching the entire scene from a distance when he received the 911 to get back to the Westside. He and the crew jumped back in their cars and headed back to the house.

____

While in the linen closet with Pete, I could sense that dark presence again. The last time I felt its presence I never saw its face. It was just an image in a dark hooded cape. This time I saw its face. It looked like the dark creatures of my dreams. Its face was that of an ugly beast—one with the resemblance of a leopard, with eyes red like fire and large massive feet like a bear with claws of sharp razors, protruding from its feet. Its mouth was shaped like a lion, capable of devouring anything in a single gesture.[8]

As I stared at it unafraid, it uttered these words: "Today I will mark you[9] as my war baby. You can do nothing unless I authorize it. I am the unholy trinity and you will worship me, for I have all power over you. I have made you to curse God and to carry the number 666,[10] and you will only go where I send you."

As quickly as it appeared, it vanished before me.

Pete asked, "Man, what were you staring at?"

"Absolutely nothing. Can you call the guys in?" I asked.

"Uh, sure," Pete said reluctantly.

____

[8] Revelation 13:2, NIV
[9] Revelation 13:16, NIV
[10] Revelation 13:18, NIV

Chump and the rest of Pete's men arrived at the house. I instructed them to form a circle and place their hands on each other's shoulders. They all looked at each other like I had lost my mind. Guys, I'm going to pray:

Dear Lord, we stand here in solidarity. We didn't ask for the war but it has found us. I am sorry for all the bad things I said to you, about you and to others about you. Please forgive us of our sins. Know that we are fighting not because we want to but because the fight has come to us. Your Word says that we are yours and we have the power to overcome the antichrist. He came here today but I proclaim that your Spirit is in me and that your Spirit is greater than the spirit of this world.[11] God grant us victory. Please go by Amityville Baptist Church and bring comfort to those who have lost someone they love. Be with Pastor Dick and his family in Jesus' name I pray. Amen!"

All the guys chimed in with a hearty "Amen!" Pete then instructed the guys to get in position, acknowledging that all the surveillance cameras around the property were in working order. As the men positioned themselves for war, Sleezie showed up. No one had seen the surveillance footage except me and Pete. All the guys started high-fiving each other as they updated Sleezie on what was taking place. I

---

[11] 1 John 4:4, NIV

grabbed Sleezie before he could get too comfortable and slammed him against the wall.

"You're a traitor!"

"Hey man, what are you saying? You're the one who brought trouble into the camp, not me!" Sleezie responded.

Without saying a word, Pete pointed his gun at Sleezie and shot him in the foot. Not understanding what was going on, the guys were speechless.

"Who are you?" Pete shouted, shooting Sleezie in the leg.

The guys started to come to Sleezie's defense but I put up my hand to stop them.

"He killed Charlie!" I said calmly.

"I said, who are you?" Pete shouted, shooting Sleezie in his other leg.

"Ok, ok man." Sleezie relented, "I'm the Chancellor's nephew!"

Pete and I looked at each other completely stunned by that revelation.

"I took you in when nobody else wanted you." Pete said.

"I fed you and made you who you are. I even gave you Zeke's bed to sleep in and this is how you repay me?"

Pete was about to shoot Sleezie again when I grabbed his arm.

"Pete, wait a minute!" I said. "Sleezie, tell us what's going on? Is the Chancellor still alive?"

Sleezie refused to answer. Pete aimed his gun and shot off one of his ears. Sleezie started screaming as Pete aimed the gun in his face.

"Ok, I'll tell you everything! Please don't shoot me again!" Sleezie pleaded.

"We are listening!" I said.

"When the Chancellor found out I was staying here with you he made me promise to be his informant. If I didn't do what he wanted he threatened to kill my momma. I thought the Chancellor was joking until he sent one of his guys to his sister's house. The Chancellor is crazy! I told him I would do whatever he wanted me to do. About two months ago, he sent me over to that Baptist Church in Amityville and told me I had to pop off the Pastor's wife and make it look like an accident. He then forced me to set up Zeke. I made sure he had the apple juice he needed. Before he knew it, Zeke was in so deep that he couldn't afford to pay for it. The Chancellor had me organize the shoot-out. I never wanted to kill Zeke! He was like a brother to me!" cried Sleezie.

Pete walked away so no one could see him cry.

"Danny, can I get some water man? My mouth is dry" Sleezie pleaded.

"Man, you better swallow and talk faster!" I said.

"Danny, the Chancellor was the one who ordered the hit on the church last night but I made an anonymous call to the Pastor. I pretended that I was from the rehab center and told him that he had better come over quickly because Chelsea was asking for her sisters! You hear me, Danny? Look, I couldn't allow any more innocent people to be killed!" Sleezie said, feeling a bit of remorse from all the tragedy he had caused.

I felt a sense of relief knowing the truth but there were a lot of people in the church that I knew very well; and it pained me to think about how they had lost their lives.

"Why did you shoot Charlie?" I yelled.

"I had to." Sleezie said.

"She came into the kitchen and I didn't know how much she had heard. The Chancellor told me to kill her or he would kill me! Look, the Chancellor is planning a hit on us around sunset. He asked me to keep y'all in the house until he arrived." Sleezie grimaced, as he recanted the Chancellor's instructions.

The pain of it all was evident all over Sleezie's face and he was sweating profusely.

"Where is Chancellor, now?" I shouted.

"I'm not sure. Listen, all I know is that you put out a hit on him the other night on the Eastside and now he's coming for you!" Sleezie cried.

"What time did you say he was coming?" Pete asked.

"Man, he told me at sunset!" Sleezie replied.

"So, we have about an hour to sunset, right? You better be telling the truth Sleezie," Pete yelled.

"Man, I wouldn't lie to you! I'm so sorry. Can I get some…"

A deafening shot rang out. Pete had put a bullet right in the middle of Sleezie's head.

"Get him out of my kitchen!" Pete shouted to his guys.

Pete made a call to check to see how close his Eastside comrades were and told them to stay on the periphery and not come near the house. They were approximately five minutes from the house. Just as Pete hung up all hell had broken loose. The Chancellor was already outside and had taken out three of Pete's seven men.

Pete looked at me and said, "I want you to take position in the hideout since it is a vantage point. You can see the whole front of the house from there. The three of us will hold the fort here. I will call my comrades and tell them the fight has begun!"

As I ran up the stairs, I looked back at Pete and said another quick prayer asking God for his safekeeping. Pete had stopped to make the call. By the time I reached the hideout, I saw Pete walking out the door like Rambo. He didn't stand a chance. The Chancellor and his gang shot him dead on the spot. They were all celebrating but what they did not realize is the celebration was a bit premature. The Eastside comrades rained in so much firepower that the cars disintegrated. I quickly realized that Pete had sent me to a place of safety. I fell on my knees, thanking God for fighting this war while realizing that we were still not out of the woods yet.

The one thing we had not contemplated was the depth of the Chancellor's evil roots. He still managed the foster home so it was a way to keep warm bodies fighting for his cause. I could hear police and ambulance sirens in the distance. I slipped through the underground tunnel that led from the hideout to Liza's Deli on Main. I left Wyandanch that evening and headed back to Amityville.

WHEN PEACE KNOCKS

The quiet unassuming community of Amityville was rocked to its core over the senseless loss of life and burning of the Amityville Baptist Church. The flames were so intense that it took the fire department well over an hour to put the flames out. Pastor Dick, along with his church members and a growing crowd of local spectators, supporters and onlookers, stood behind a yellow barricade tape praying for survivors. But as they watched the church being leveled to a heap of ash, it was highly unlikely there would be any survivors. When the fire department finally exhumed what bodies they could find, they only discovered eleven—eleven bodies which had been burned well beyond recognition. At this point, everyone's heart sank. Only an autopsy would be able to confirm the identity of the poor souls who had lost their lives in the fire.

Pastor Dick stood frozen in place, dumbfounded and at a loss for words for what to say to his congregants. Not long after, Sis. Sheila Schmidt, the choir director and musician had arrived. Distraught over what she was seeing, Sis. Schmidt collapsed; overwhelmed by the senseless loss of life of people she once knew. Several church members held on to her, trying to console and comfort her. She had every right to be distraught because her husband, Deacon Schmidt, and her two youngest sons (who had insisted on supporting their dad) were among the fatalities.

"Oh my God!" one of the firemen yelled. "Somebody get one of the paramedics over here right now!"

Underneath two badly charred bodies was a ten-year old boy with second and third degree burns on his arms and legs. His face had barely been touched and was covered with smoke.

"Get out of the way folks! Let the paramedics through!" the fireman shouted.

Pastor Dick ran alongside the stretcher carrying young Samuel. His eyes widened with excitement and shock:

"Oh my God, Sis. Sheila, it's Samuel! Samuel is alive!"

Pastor Dick raised his hands towards heaven. "Lord, thank you! Thank you for saving Samuel's life!"

Amid so much tragedy the Lord had given the people a ray of hope, which gave way to a moment of joyous thanksgiving and celebration of life.

I arrived shortly after the discovery of little Samuel. The grounds of the church looked worse than a war zone—more like hell than anything else. The stench from the burning flesh literally turned my stomach. All I could do is fall to my knees, crying out to God and asking for forgiveness.

I was so engrossed in this repetitive prayer that I did not notice Melissa, Courtney and Maddy running towards me. They were all screaming, crying and calling out my name, "Danny, Danny!" I looked up and the three of them jumped into my arms. I was so relieved to see them. When I looked up Pastor Dick was less than pleased.

"Melissa, Courtney and Maddy, please wait in the car for me." Pastor Dick said. They left and went to the car as their father instructed.

"Dad, please let me explain!" I said.

It was the first time I had ever called him dad. He was equally shocked but before I could say another word, he said:

"Son, evil follows you and it goes before you because you are a war baby!"

"Look what your actions have done to this church, community and me," Pastor Dick yelled. "You have to go, Daniel. Please go as far as possible away from me and the rest of my family."

**Evil is like an adhesive. As it sticks to you
it will travel wherever you go**.

"So, are you saying that I am no longer part of the family?" I asked.

"Son, you will always have a place in my heart but you can't stay here. You have to go!" Pastor Dick said sternly.

I realized that night, that I had never grieved before. When Deb shot dad, momma and herself, I never cried. When my best friend Zeke was shot and killed, I never cried. When Charlotte, Pete and the gang was shot, I never cried. I shed a tear or two, when I got the news about the church, but I never really cried. I realized that over the years my heart had become a heart of stone. The hurt ran so deeply, I couldn't cry for all the bad things my dad said to me as a young boy. All the women I had slept with—all the fancy clothes and cars—had never touched my heart 'cause they were just things.

For every war that engaged me and every war that I engaged, they had hardened my heart. I did not care anymore. I did not allow anyone or anything to invade my space so I could love. In the beginning before war I loved my momma but she was taken from me. I loved my sister Deb and she was taken from me. The Therault family found me, took me in but I could not take them in, take in their kindness, compassion or love.

Who am I? What have I become? I marvel at everyone's philosophy of what is required to become successful. I have attained and yet I do not feel successful. My world is a closed book and I have become the one thing I never wanted to be—a causality of war. The family motto says *one must fight in order to be free.* I have fought and what did it do for me? Nothing! Nothing more can fit into my life and it is too full to take anything out. I hate what and who I have become. The very people who love me who are left, I have hurt. Pastor Dick's words, reverberated in my ears, "Son, evil has followed you and gone before you, you are a war baby." I AM A WAR BABY!

Intertwined at the door stands mediocrity and yet broader more distinctive opportunities. Two choices present themselves—mediocrity and opportunity—but between the two is war. A war that causes even the strongest personality to submit to the inferior characteristics. War is encountered more frequently than one would like. We can either allow it to consume us through self-destruction or propel us through a trajectory of supernatural proportion.

A war baby's life is bitter, typically caused by someone else's bitterness. We are a singled-out culture that rests in conflicting positions that are colored by a pen called "perceived harmony." It destroyed and killed my sister Deb; it destroyed momma as she became clouded by the façade of her husband (my dad); and Ms. Maddy and the church members became a physical casualty of it.

**Be a war baby but fight the good fight.
Stand against evil.**

As I drove off from the scene of the burning church, I pulled over into the layby and cried. "God, I just want to die!" As the tears streamed down my face, I began to sob so hard that the jolts from my body caused a terrible pain near my lungs, causing me to collapse. I was told later that a passerby saw my lights on and engine still running, and came over to check on me. They found me in a slumped position over the steering wheel. When I woke up I was in the Intensive Care Unit at the Amityville Hospital.

The attending nurse called out, "Doctor, he's awake!"

Dr. Westmund entered my room not looking at all positive. So, I jokingly asked, "Doc, am I going to live?"

Dr. Westmund was the Senior Attending Doctor for the Intensive Care Unit. He also attended to me the first time I was brought to the hospital.

He looked at me and said, "Mr. Schmartz, when you abruptly left the hospital a few days ago, we were not able to tell you the seriousness of your injury. You were shot in your left shoulder and in your abdomen. When we went in to operate we identified a few things. Let me ask you this: Have you experienced pains in your chest, loss of breath or fatigue before?"

Sarcastically, I responded, "Yeah doc, when I was about fourteen or fifteen years old but the doctors said it was because of the trauma I had gone through."

"May I ask, what type of trauma?"

"Well, when I was around ten years old I watched my sister shoot my dad, my mom and then she turned the gun on herself."

"Oh, my goodness!" Doctor Westmund said, "I'm so sorry for your loss."

"Hey Doc, life happens," I said casually. "So, why you askin' me 'bout my shortness of breath?"

"Mr. Schmartz, in addition to your gunshot wounds, we discovered that you were probably born with a genetic defect called aortic stenosis. This is an obstruction in the aorta that restricts the steady flow of blood into the heart. As you are probably aware, the aorta carries oxygen-rich blood to the body. Over the years, the obstruction has placed a serious strain on your heart function. When the bullet hit your shoulder, it tore up several blood vessels and tissue in the chest area. We were only able to remove pieces of the bullet from your shoulder." said Dr. Westmund, "The first time you were admitted we were unable to extract the live bullet lodged in your abdomen. We knew that it could detonate at any time. So, our initial approach was to place you in a self-induced coma to keep you immobile but when you came to, you discharged yourself."

"Yeah doc, sometimes a man got to do what a man got to do. Perhaps sacrifice comes with the territory."

"Tell me Mr. Schmartz, I see in your chart that you were born in 1975. Is that correct?"

"Yeah, and your point is?" I said.

"Mr. Schmartz, my son would have been the same age you are now had he lived but a drunk driver killed both him and his mother when he was only thirteen."

"Mr. Schmartz, may I call you Daniel?"

"Sure doc, that's fine!"

"Daniel, you seem to be a very intelligent young man. Sounds like you made a few bad decisions along the way. I find that when our heavenly Father gives us a second chance at life that we must do everything in our power to do things differently."

"Listen, three days ago you were found slumped over the steering wheel of your car. The live bullet from your abdomen dislodged itself, travelled to your left bronchial area and exploded. Your left lung was totally severed."

"We were able to patch up your lung. But my real concern is that the shrapnel from the bullet has splintered and is now traveling through your blood stream."

"Daniel, your days are literally numbered." Dr. Westmund said.

"Wow, so what happens now?" I asked.

"We are going to try and stabilize you but we will need to keep you confined to this hospital bed until we can determine our next move."

"Do you mean indefinitely?" I said.

"Well, all I can say for now is try and get comfortable."

Dr. Westmund patted me on the shoulder and left the room. It had been a long day and I was exhausted. As I drifted off to sleep I had the dream again:

I was home in the living room with my family. I walked into the kitchen to get something from the fridge but when I turned around I couldn't get back to the living room. The kitchen floor had opened and I saw what appeared to be hell with the lake of fire in the midst of it. Everything was burning and the heat coming from it was burning me. Since the hole was not that big, I thought I could jump across it to reach the other side. But when I jumped the hole became wider than in my previous dreams. Something very powerful was pulling me down into the hole as I dangled off the edge with the grips of my fingers. I was screaming for help and saw momma, Deb, dad, Ms. Maddy and Pastor Dick but they wouldn't help me. They just stared at me. I screamed again and this time a huge hand (like a man's hand) grabbed me. I never saw a face or body but I heard a voice. He said, "Not Daniel, he's mine! Now release him." The hole in the kitchen floor that tried to swallow me, ejected me and slowly began to close.

This time when I woke up I remembered I was not afraid but at peace. As I lay in the hospital bed, I thought to myself, "Man you are twenty-four years old and have been given another opportunity. Ya gotta put things right."

WHAT DO YOU SEE?

When Pastor Dick told me to leave, his words and actions forced me to come to grips with my life, who I was and everything I stood for. Sometimes the greatest lessons are learned through the hardship of our own experiences. Confined to a hospital bed for two months forced me to think. Nothing had changed with me physically but everything had changed with me spiritually and emotionally because I rediscovered my faith.

Lessons that shape our character hinge on impactful life experiences.

As painful as it was I had not spoken to Pastor Dick since he told me to leave. I resolved within myself that as soon as I was well enough to leave the hospital I would find a way to heal our broken relationship. I truly missed my family. As I strategized on how to make amends, I received a surprising visit from Chelsea Therault:

"Hey Danny, may I come in?" Chelsea asked as she approached my bed.

My eyes lit up when I saw her. She looked so good and it was nice to know that the old habit of us intruding on each other's privacy had not changed.

"Sure, pull up a chair. You are looking well," I commented.

"Yep. I've completed my rehabilitation program and have been drug-free for three months now." she said, giving me a thumbs up.

"I am a recovering addict and I know that I will always be one but I've recommitted my life to the Lord. Now, I serve in ministry alongside my daddy."

"Melissa is a junior in high school now and both Courtney and Maddy are in middle school."

"Chelsea, I need to say something first."

The guilt of everything that I had done was gnawing at me. I wanted to apologize but before I could utter another word, Chelsea put her hand up as if to signal that she was not finished talking yet.

"Danny, I forgive you and thank you."

"Forgive me? For what?"

"What possible reason could you have for wanting to thank me?"

Chelsea seemed lost in her own thoughts. Out of respect, I remained silent while waiting on her to speak. Reaching for my hand, she gently clasped my hand and placed into hers:

"Danny, let me start by saying it makes it easier for me to say what's on my heart by starting with a simple thank you."

"Dad told me that you found me on Main Street in Wyandanch doing some things that I'm not very proud of. I'm not sure if I can fully explain why I was there or what my reasons were for putting myself in that situation. But what I do know is that I am truly thankful to you that you had the instincts to follow the car I was in and bring me back to Amityville, despite being shot." Chelsea said. "You told the nurse who I was so they could call my dad. That whole scenario could have turned out so differently had you not been there for me. So, thank you for everything, Danny!"

Chelsea gently caressed and patted my hand. I so wanted to express how undeserving I was of her kindness and compassion but she again raised her hand to stop me from talking. For what seemed like an eternity, Chelsea sat back in her seat, staring at me in silence with those kind baby blue eyes. It was the first time I had noticed how much she had changed. I had to choke back the tears because she looked so much like her mother, Ms. Maddy.

"Danny, I know the whole story about my mom." she said. "When mommy was hit by that drunk driver my whole life changed. You know what it's like to lose someone near and dear to your heart; that person who cradles you in their arms and comforts you through all the minor cuts, scrapes and broken heart stories."

By now, both Chelsea and I had tears streaming down our faces. There was an unspoken language between us as if we were trying to console each through our tears.

"When you love someone that much and they are taken from you it hurts twice as much." Chelsea said.

My insides began to shudder and I felt increasingly sick to my stomach.

"Danny?" Chelsea said softly.

"Yes, Chelsea." I answered.

"Danny, I know my mother was the victim of a crime that was not necessarily orchestrated by you but orchestrated because of you." she said. "I know you wouldn't intentionally hurt my mommy or our family. That is why I can genuinely say from my heart that I forgive you. But the real reason I am here is to tell you to forgive yourself, so forgiveness can heal your heart too!"

————————

**No matter how deep the inflicted pain is,
learn to forgive.**

————————

I turned my head and looked out the hospital window. Her words pierced my heart. My mind was racing but my heart was still. I wanted to forgive myself but didn't know where to start. Even more, I wanted to respond but I couldn't find the words. As I turned to looked at her, the only thing I could think of was how hard all of this was for me:

"Danny, I know what you are thinking." Chelsea stated. "You are asking yourself, how do I receive forgiveness? Well, it all starts with you first learning to forgive yourself."

"How in the world did you know what I am thinking?"

"Because not too long ago I was in the same place you are now." she said.

"Danny, after mommy died I hated life and I especially hated myself. I got caught up in drugs, alcohol, illicit sex, stealing, lying and cheating, and I became a victim of a war. I blamed everyone for what was happening to me. Then one day my social worker, Bethany Stoneham, came into my room and changed my life forever. Boy, she had the most unorthodox way of teaching, so she hands me a mirror!"

"A mirror?' I asked.

"Yes, a mirror."

"I asked Ms. Bethany, "Why in the world are you handing me a mirror?'

She said, "Look in it."

"I yelled at her and said, 'I don't need no stupid mirror! I know what I look like!' So, I threw the mirror on the floor. Over the course of the next week, she would bring me a mirror every day and every day I would throw it on the floor."

"Man, she must've had a lot of mirrors," I said.

"Never thought of it like that," responded Chelsea.

"Yeah, she came to my room about six times. On the seventh time, she handed me the mirror but she held onto it. Ms. Bethany said, "Chelsea Therault, I am asking you to look in the mirror. When I finally looked in the mirror, she asked me the dumbest thing ever. She said what do you see? And I said, 'Me, of course, and boy do I look like crap!'"

"She asked me again, what do you see Chelsea? I said, well my hair isn't combed. I look awful without makeup and I have a pimple on my face."

"For a third time she said, Chelsea what do you see? I broke down and started crying. Through all my tears, I said I see nothing. Ms. Bethany then said, great! Now here is what I see. I see the face of a beautiful young lady, with exceptional ability and purpose. I see a person who is infused with greatness. I see a person who has the ability through her experiences to change the world!"

When you hold the mirror, you have an opportunity to capture what is seen.

"I shifted my glance from the mirror to Ms. Bethany: You really see all that in me? She said, 'Yes I do and so much more. But before you can see it Chelsea, you must first learn to forgive yourself. Only then will your eyes be opened to the predestined greatness inside of you.'"

"Danny, no one had ever said anything like that to me before. I suddenly realized that fear and hurt had kept me from believing in who I am." Chelsea said, patting her chest near her heart as if to suggest that change must begin within the heart. "It was so much easier for me to blame everyone else for my shortcomings."

"Chelsea, may I share something with you? I have never shared this with anybody before."

"Sure, fire a way!" Chelsea said.

"What a choice of words," I thought to myself. "Ok, so shortly before my family died I started having these dreams. The dreams were always fragmented, they came in two parts. There is one dream I continue to have repeatedly. Each time I have this one particular dream I would wake up terrified and afraid but the last time I had it I was not afraid at all."

I was home in the living room with my family. I walked into the kitchen to get something from the fridge but when I turned around I couldn't get back to the living room. The kitchen floor had opened and I saw what appeared to be hell with the lake of fire in the midst of it. Everything was burning and the heat coming from it was burning me. Since the hole was not that big, I thought I could jump over it to reach the other side. But when I jumped, the hole became wider than all the previous times. Something very powerful was pulling me down into the hole as I dangled off the edge of the hole with only the tips of my fingers. I was screaming for help. I saw momma, Deb and dad but they wouldn't help me, they just stared at me. I screamed again and this huge hand (like a man's hand) grabbed me. I never saw a face or body. I only heard a voice saying, 'Not Daniel, he's mine! Now release him.' The hole in the kitchen floor that tried to swallow me, ejected me and slowly began to close.

"Then I had this vision where I encountered a dark presence just before the big fight at Pete's house. *It* said to me, "I have power over you and you will only go where and when I send you!"

I asked what *it* wanted from me and *it* said, "I am the unholy trinity. Those who think they know me refer to me as the Antichrist but that is not who I am. I am your savior, the one who provided you with riches, fame and even life. I am the beast who has control over you, Chelsea, Pastor Dick and anyone you regard as a friend. I have made you my war baby and now you belong to me."

Chelsea sat in silence, appearing lost in her own thoughts. She was staring out the hospital window as if her answer was outside somewhere.

"Chelsea, did you hear what I said?"

Chelsea pulled out her phone and pulls up her Bible app.

"Danny, I want to read you a couple of scriptures that will help you understand your dreams. The first one is found in the twelfth chapter of John:

So Jesus said to them, "For a little while longer the Light is among you. Walk while you have the Light, so that darkness will not overtake you; he who walks in the darkness does not know where he goes. While you have the Light, believe in the Light, so that you may become sons of Light." These things Jesus spoke, and He went away and hid Himself from them. [12]

"Jesus spoke these words to the crowds and His followers to explain the motive behind his death and what He expected of those He was leaving behind after His departure. What Jesus was trying to tell them is that they would only have Him (the Light) for a brief period and at some point, they will find themselves stumbling in darkness.

---

[12] John 12:35-36, NAS

The one thing He wanted to make absolutely clear to them and us is, that no matter what trials or challenges we go through, we must always put our trust and confidence in Him; for we are His sons and daughters and we serve as reflections of His light." Chelsea said. "Danny, we both were brought up in the ways of the Lord but the darkness overtook us because of the choices we made. We chose to live differently from what we knew was right. Now, imagine what we could have been had we followed the example and teachings of Christ? We chose to walk in darkness as if we were impervious and oblivious to His light. Do you agree?"

"Yeah, I do actually," I replied.

Chelsea continues: "So, this is what I believe the Lord is trying to reveal to you through your dreams: I believe, the dream concerning the kitchen floor opening up and revealing the lake of fire and hell is to show you the outcome of your life if you continue on the path you are on. When a person thinks they will never be caught, their evil deeds continue because their motives have not changed. We see this type of mindset in the body of Christ (the spiritual church) of today. However, to be the type of church that reflects the Light, we must follow the example of Christ (the true and living Way), as we immerse ourselves in the Word of God. Unfortunately, Danny, what we say is not always what we do. We believe our actions do not hurt anyone but in the long run it does. Take the two of us for example. Our lives are less than what they should have been because of our poor choices. We have hurt, even destroyed, the lives of so many people while we remained shrouded under the notion that no one sees us. The one thing we both forgot is that God sees and knows all things. So, when you tried to jump over the lake of fire and failed to make it, God was revealing to you just how far off the beaten path you have gone. Think about it, Danny. If you had made the jump in your dreams, then we probably would not be having this conversation. Does any of this make sense to you Danny?"

"Yeah, sort of."

"Ok, what part is not very clear to you?" Chelsea asked.

"Chelsea, almost everything that has happened was not even my fault. I didn't look for war, it found me. It found me when I was ten years old. Everywhere I go it always finds me!"

"Danny, when you look in the mirror what do you see?"

"Me of course."

"Are you sure?" Chelsea asked.

"Here's my compact mirror. Look in the mirror and tell me everything you see."

"I see part of the hospital bed and my pillow."

"Great!" said Chelsea. "Now what is the most dominant thing you see in the mirror?"

"Me, Chelsea. I told you that already."

"Then ask yourself, why have you allowed the smaller insignificant things that you see to overshadow the larger major thing in the mirror?"

"Huh?"

"Danny, we are so quick as adults to allow the actions and conversations of others to dictate our behavior. Especially when we know good and well that it is not right or in our best interests. Then when things start to fall apart, we want to blame everyone else but ourselves! Do you remember the song recorded by Michael Jackson called 'Man in the Mirror?' Chelsea giggled as she sang a couple verses of the song:

> I'm starting with the man in the mirror
> I'm asking him to change his ways
> And no message could have been any clearer
> If you want to make the world a better place
> Take a look at yourself and make that change[13]

We both giggled over her singing. I had never heard Chelsea sing before but she was amazing!

---

[13] Lyric excerpts from the album "Bad 25" produced by Universal Music Publishing Group. Lead Vocalist, Michael Jackson in collaboration with Siedah Garrett, The Winans and the Andrae Crouch Choir. Retrieved from https://binged.it/2osSxN6.

"Girl, you've got some lungs on you!" I commented.

"Thanks," Chelsea said, quickly moving back to the discussion at hand.

"So, the last part of your dream really sticks out to me, Danny."

"How's that?"

"You said, a huge hand like a man's hand grabbed you but I never saw the face or body of the person. But then you heard the person say, 'No, not Daniel! He's mine. Now release him' and then the hole slowly began to close.' That is so powerful Danny!"

"The second scripture I want to share with you is from the thirteenth chapter of Revelation:"

It was given power to wage war against God's holy people and to conquer them. And it was given authority over every tribe, people, language and nation. All inhabitants of the earth will worship the beast—all whose names have not been written in the Lamb's book of life, the Lamb who was slain from the creation of the world. Whoever has ears, let them hear…This calls for patient endurance and faithfulness on the part of God's people.[14]

"Danny, the dark presence in your vision who spoke to you was the beast messing with your psyche. Unfortunately, he had you in his grips for a long time because of your

---

[14] Revelation 13:7-10b, NIV

lifestyle. But you must also realize that it was given permission to address you, to try and confuse and frighten you." Chelsea said. "Remember the huge hand that pulled you out and the voice that said, 'Daniel is mine, now release him,' and *it* did as it was commanded? Well that was Jesus Christ. You must realize that you are His and that He loves you so much, despite everything you have done. He died so that you would not have to die in sin! Oh Danny, he loves you so much!" Chelsea said. "Danny, do you love Him?"

**Know that Satan is defeated.
Walk in that assurance.**

"Oh, so I finally get to talk, huh?" I said sarcastically. "Just before you showed up today, I was contemplating how to get right with God, Pastor Dick, you, Melissa, Courtney and Maddy. The five of you are the only family I have but I don't know where to begin or what to do?"

"Well, confession *is* good for the soul when it comes to healing the heart." Chelsea said.

"Danny, I know I told you I was only going to read two scriptures but there is one other passage that I want to share with you. I promise, this will be the last one. Let's read this one together, ok?" Chelsea shows Daniel her phone and they begin reciting the passage together:

But what does it say? "The word is near you; it is in your mouth and in your heart," that is, the message concerning faith that we proclaim: If you declare with your mouth, "Jesus is Lord," and believe in your heart that God raised him from the dead, you will be saved. For it is with your heart that you believe and are justified, and it is with your mouth that you profess your faith and are saved. As Scripture says, "Anyone who believes in him will never be put to shame." For there is no difference between Jew and Gentile—the same Lord is Lord of all and richly blesses all who call on him, for, "Everyone who calls on the name of the Lord will be saved."[15]

"Do you believe this Danny?" Chelsea asked.

Involuntary tears started to roll down my cheeks. I have been doing a lot of crying lately but this time it felt good.

"Yes, Chelsea, I do believe it."

"Good. So, let's pray together. Repeat these words after me."

"Dear Lord, I admit that I am a sinner. I have done many things that didn't please you. All my life, I have lived for myself only and in the process I have hurt many people that I love, especially you. I am so sorry, I repent of my sins and I am asking you Lord

---

[15] Romans 10:8-13, NIV

to please forgive me. I believe that you died on the cross for my sins and to save me. You did what I could not do for myself. I come to you now, asking you to take control of my life. I give myself and my life to you. From this day forward, help me to live every day for you in a way that pleases you. I love you, Lord, and thank you, in Jesus' name, Amen."

"Danny, today is a new beginning for you! One other thing, I need to tell you. By the time I leave you today, the devil may try and convince you otherwise but know by faith that you are saved. Allow God to help you, to lead and guide you. Also, and I'm not sure why I'm saying this but, listen to Him in the claps of thunder! Wow, I don't know where that came from but I hope it makes sense to you."

I looked at her. How did Chelsea know to say those exact words?

"Well, Danny, I have to run. Do you need anything? Will you be ok here alone in the hospital?"

"Sure." I said.

"Ok, well call me if you need anything. Love you bro."

With these parting words, Chelsea kissed me on the forehead and left.

Imagine that. Chelsea had called me her brother. As I settled into the pillow behind my head, I smiled to myself. I was exhausted but I had never felt so good in my entire life. With that thought, I slowly drifted off to sleep.

As Chelsea got in her car, she was deeply troubled by the last part of her brother's words and his encounter with a dark presence. She wrestled with the words: "I am the beast and I have control over you, Chelsea, Pastor Dick and all whom you call friend. I have made you my war baby and now you belong to me." Chelsea had an uncanny feeling there was something behind the words and it left her feeling extremely uneasy and uncomfortable, which is why she intentionally did not interpret Danny's dream for him. This was something worthy of prayer and seeking the Lord for greater clarity.

HUMBLE BEGINNINGS

The time spent in a hospital had given me pause to reflect. I thought about the community of Amityville and all the members of Amityville Baptist Church. They were a strong people and everything they had encountered only served to bring them closer together. This newfound trajectory of excellence that they all embraced was something only those who aspire to be sons and daughters of the Light could experience.

Pastor Richard ("Dick") Therault always felt deeply humbled and honored to serve as Amityville Baptist Church's pastor. The community rallied around him, pouring their love into the Therault family. Collectively, the church and community became a cohesive society—a society of "the called" individuals, drawing strength from the audible messages of *The Way* versus the noise of those who stand on the periphery of the claps of thunder.

Prior to that fatal Bible study night, when so many of his parishioners had lost their lives, the church's attendance was around twenty-five people, which included Pastor Dick, Ms. Maddy, Chelsea, Melissa, Courtney, Maddy and me. If you excluded the entire Therault family, then realistically there was technically only 19 members of the church in total. Post to the fatal tragedy, the church began to grow exponentially.

It had been two months since that horrific ordeal and everyone in the community was trying to piece their lives back together after the tragedy. So many people had lost their lives on that dreadful Tuesday evening. War does not discriminate. It brings with it casualties that include both the innocent and guilty. By the same token, it can also humble us, bringing us to a place of repentance in submission to a sovereign God—a God who faithfully heals, delivers, protects and provides for a chosen people. I understood the nature of war because I had experienced it for myself. Chelsea kept me informed of all that was happening in Amityville while I was incapacitated.

There was one small miracle, little Samuel Schmidt. He had already undergone four surgeries due to the severity of his burns. The doctors confirmed to his mother that he would make a complete recovery, scarred but not impacted physically.

____

**War doesn't discriminate.
It captures both the guilty and the innocent.**

____

Chelsea shared with me that it felt like the church had a funeral every other day until all were laid to rest. Her dad was trying to have one large funeral but the eleven families of the deceased were resistant, and so one by one he laid them to rest. It was both an exhausting and testing time for her father.

———————

"Danny, this whole ordeal has taken a toll on dad. His whole persona is becoming dark. Almost nightly, he pours himself a drink and when I questioned him about his actions, he says, 'I am simply trying to take the edge off.'" Chelsea said. "I'm concerned, Danny, that dad is becoming a closet alcoholic."

I could see the pain in her face as she continued sharing how the tragedy had affected our father, the church members and the people within the community:

"Shortly after the fatal tragedy, the governing body of the Amityville High School met with the Deacon board to offer the temporary use of its gymnasium for any future church services. What a blessing that was for everyone to hear! The first service was held on the third Sunday in September and I remember it being a beautiful Fall day in Amityville. Dad gave the most stirring sermon I had ever heard him preach."

As Pastor Dick stood to address the waiting congregation, his mind raced back and forth between the challenges of the day and the difficult struggles of the last few months.

"This has been a hellish year," Pastor Dick thought to himself.

He looked towards heaven thanking God for His grace and mercy in remaining faithful to His promise: *"Never will I leave you; never will I forsake you."*[16] As Pastor Dick looked out to the now more than 150 congregants, he said:

"I am thankful, that God is still God! Amen!"

The congregation echoed in response, "Amen!" He looked towards the piano where his wife, Ms. Maddy, would have ministered in song before he preached. He nodded his head as if to pay homage to her former presence. Turning his attention back to the congregation, he asked that they open their Bibles to Romans 8:37: *"No, in all these things we are more than conquerors through him who loved us."*

"I would like to minister to your hearts today on the topic of *Finding Value While In The Valley,*" Pastor Dick said stoically.

Chelsea recalled the atmosphere being very uplifting and electrifying, as the people sat in anticipation of what the Lord was going to say through Pastor Dick. Her father

---

[16] Hebrews 13:5b, NIV

paused for a brief minute, then looked at the waiting congregation and began to speak:

"Most of us are familiar with the story of Ruth and I would like to use that familiar story as a backdrop for my sermon today. When you get home, I encourage you to read it for yourself. You can read about Ruth's story in the Book of Ruth, chapter one, verses one through twenty-two."

Pastor Dick cleared his throat and continued speaking: "Many of us seek a mountain top experience. When everything is going good and when our home life is balanced, we are satisfied because it has the sensations of a mountain top experience. Just when everything seems to be going just right, disaster strikes. What we often forget is that for every mountain top experience, there will also be a valley experience. But it is in the valley that we learn how to not lean to our own understanding. Can I get an amen from somebody?"

"Preach, Pastor!" Deacon Menders shouted.

"Now, tell the person next to you, I'm looking for the value in the valley!"

Focusing his attention back on the story of Ruth, Pastor Dick begins to articulate his inspirational message:

"In Ruth 1:1-22, we come across two individuals named Naomi and Elimelech. During the rule of the Judges, Israel suffered a serious famine, which was deemed to be one of the punishments visited upon the people by God when they had sinned.[17] Elimelech decided to migrate with his family to another land where the food was more plentiful. And so, they traveled from Bethlehem-Judah to settle in the highlands of Moab."

"Uprooting from her native home must have been a real sacrifice for Naomi. Sincere in her faith, she loved the people of God and was strongly attached to the wonderful traditions of her race. But when Elimelech took his family to Moab, he stepped outside the will of God. Famine was the consequence and judgment God placed upon the nation of Israel for their disobedience."

"Instead of running away from the problem, Elimelech should have repented and turned to God. Naturally speaking, it made sense for Elimelech to uproot his family and reestablish them in a place where the struggle was not as great and the food was more plentiful. Let's bring this a little closer to home so we can relate to it. Whenever a person goes through a valley experience, it is always wise to remain faithful to God and steadfast in the belief that He can and

---

[17] Leviticus 26:14, 16

will deliver you out of and bring you through the situation," Pastor Dick said.

"Elimelech was a Hebrew who abided under God's promise, "in the days of famine they shall be satisfied."[18] Moreover, the name Elimelech means "my God is King." Had Elimelech truly believed and regarded God as King, then he would have stayed in Bethlehem-Judah, exercising the faith that God would supply the necessary provisions for he and his family."

"Naomi found herself in a valley experience through no fault of her own. She must have felt out-of-sorts being in a strange land while trying to establish a home in repellant surroundings. She was a woman of faith and she loved her God. But she was in a place that did not support her faith. Her sons had intermingled and married Moabite women which was something the Jewish law forbade. Instead of supporting her after their father's death, they chose wives from an alien country—a country that was alien to their Jewish beliefs, traditions and laws."

"After the death of her husband and two sons, Naomi finds herself living in an anti-God environment with no support to sustain her. She is now old, helpless, husbandless,

---

[18] Psalm 37:19, KJV

son-less and has the burden of two daughters-in-laws, Ruth and Orpah, to shelter. True to its name, Moab was an empty, desolate and inhospitable place for Naomi's grief-stricken heart. As she and Ruth prepared to embark on a journey to return to Bethlehem-Judah, their emotions must have been overwhelming. Naomi probably reflected on earlier times when life was bountiful, balanced and happy. She may have even fantasized what life might have been like had her husband and sons not died."

"When the storms of life come our way—when we no longer experience mountain top experiences—we may feel as if the bottom has fallen out of life. We may look up from the valley and see the beauty and majesty of the mountains and begin to reflect on the times of peace, joy and happiness. We may wake up and all we can see is how far we have fallen. We may find ourselves becoming bitter, even if only for a fleeting moment. We may even become like Naomi who insisted that her friends and neighbors no longer call her by her real name (Naomi) but by the name "Mara" (meaning "bitter"), which described her emotional and psychological condition.

> *"Don't call me Naomi," she told them. "Call me Mara, because the Almighty has made my life very bitter. I went away full, but the LORD has brought me back empty. Why call me Naomi? The LORD*

has afflicted me; the Almighty has brought misfortune upon me."[19]

Pastor Dick continues, "We experienced a horrific travesty at Amityville Baptist Church. It was an experience that no one should ever have had to go through. We lost family members and church property. The hurt that we all feel is beyond any adjective we can find in the English dictionary."

Pastor Dick paused for a few minutes glancing towards the seat near the piano where his beloved wife Maddy once sat. Chelsea found herself reminiscing about her mommy too. "I miss her so much," she thought, "If she were here, she would know exactly what everyone was feeling and how to console them in the process. Pastor Dick cleared his throat, drank some water and then continued with his sermon:

"There will be times when we find ourselves in the valley but look up, church! If you can look up, you can get up because there is value in the valley experience!"

"Amen, Pastor!" the congregation shouted and applauded.

"So, how do we find value in the valley experience when it hurts this bad? As Believers, we must recognize that valley experiences are a part of our growth. It is only when we look

---

[19] Ruth 1:20-21, NIV

up and keep our focus on Jesus that we are equipped to survive and grow through it."

"Look at us! We are here and we are still alive! I don't know if Naomi recognized her value while she was going through her valley experience. But what I do know is when someone is counting on you, you don't have the time or luxury to waddle in self-pity. Naomi could have easily become self-absorbed by her own grief but she had Ruth to care for. As Ruth's mentor and example, Naomi knew that she was now responsible for Ruth. And the sheer knowledge of that gave her the incentive and motivation to live and move on!"

"I wonder how many of us have a Ruth in our lives? A Ruth that God is using to keep us from waddling in self-pity; and a Ruth who is a living testimony and agitator that propels us into the place where God wants us to live and thrive?

"Sometimes our valley experiences become challenges that we do not want to face or deal with but we are forced to endure them anyway. Sometimes those challenges can become so overwhelming that we feel as though we cannot endure another thing. Sometimes, when you go through something like we just experienced, the valley experience may not appear to have any value, purpose or meaning. You think it has no value because it is too overwhelming, it hurts too much, it feels like a stumbling block or it knocked you off course. But if you can just hold on until tomorrow, it will get better!"

Someone here today may be thinking, "Pastor, you don't understand. I don't know how much more I can take. My husband was the sole provider of our family but now he's gone. My wife knew how to keep us all together but she's gone. I gave up everything for my children and now they are gone. I honestly don't know if I can last until tomorrow. Church, let me tell you something. You have to find value in the valley experience otherwise everything you stand for is for nothing."

"The Bible says, 'The LORD will guide you always; he will satisfy your needs in a sun-scorched land and will strengthen your frame. You will be like a well-watered garden, like a spring whose waters never fail.'[20] During the low points of your journey, know that God has got your back! He will restore you like a well-watered garden and a spring whose waters never fail. Know that for every mountain there is to climb, there is a valley you must travel through. Know that God foresees every challenge in life before it occurs."

---

[20] Isaiah 58:11, NIV

"Before Naomi knew that her husband and sons would die—before she knew that she would end up in an uncomfortable place in a foreign land—God knew and saw the plans for her life. Here is the reality of Naomi's eventual mountain top experience: If her husband, Elimelech, hadn't left Bethlehem-Judah and her sons hadn't married Moabite women, then she would not have not encountered Ruth—the same Ruth who eventually married Naomi's kinsman Boaz. Through the union of Ruth and Boaz came a son named Obed. Obed was the father of Jesse, Jesse was the father of King David, and King David is a direct descendent of our Savior, Jesus Christ!"

"So, I say to you with all sincerity, find value in your valley experience! You may not understand the challenges or trials that are forced upon you. You may never know when a valley experience will occur. But you can rest assured that when and if it does come that it is designed to strengthen you, humble you and increase your faith! You will know these things when you realize who God is and that He is a faithful promise keeper."

"I want to close with a letter written by Apostle Paul while imprisoned in Rome: 'I consider that our present sufferings are not worth comparing with the glory that will be revealed in us…What, then, shall we say in response to these things? If God is for us, who can be against us? Who shall separate us from the love of Christ? Shall trouble or hardship or persecution or famine or nakedness or danger or sword? As it is written: For your sake we face death all day long; we are considered as sheep to be slaughtered, these are the valley experiences. Here's what I really want us to remember and hold on to: No, in all these things we are more than conquerors through him (Jesus Christ) who loved us![21]

"There is value in the valley experience! Let the church say, Amen!" articulated Pastor Dick. Everyone jumped to their feet and shouted with great enthusiasm, Amen!

Salvation and forgiveness is not extended via an intellectual occurrence. It happens only through the extension of faith and by the mercy of God.

It was the start of a great revival for Amityville Baptist Church. Chelsea later told me that the sermon had stirred her so deeply that it literally sparked a change deep inside of her. Not only was it the beginning of her discovering the value of her own valley experience but it also taught her the importance of forgiving those who had hurt her and how to also forgive herself. Now she could begin to heal.

---

[21] Roman 8:18, 31, 35, 37, NIV

HEART OF STONE

The Amityville Baptist Church was a steady 150 members strong. Pastor Dick determined that the time had come for them to transition from the high school gymnasium to a new church facility. The school had been extremely accommodating. Not only had they given the church access to the gymnasium for their weekly services but they also gave them access to several classrooms, which Pastor Dick had redone and converted into two offices—one for himself and Chelsea and the other for a boardroom. More than anything, he was excited to have his daughter working alongside him in ministry.

"Chelsea, please send the Deacon board a message to remind them that I need a head count on how many people are attending this evening's meeting concerning the construction of our new church facility?"

"Certainly, Pastor," Chelsea responded.

Deacon Cedric Menders was a personal confidant to Pastor Dick—the person he found comfort in being able to share his feelings and thoughts about the murder of his wife and church members. Deacon Menders had faithfully served at Amityville Baptist Church for at least eighty years and was well respected, not only in the church but the community as well. Due to his failing eyesight, he was not always present at some of the activities held in the evenings due to his impaired sight while driving. No one could out do Deacon Menders when it came to his consistency in attending the morning worship service.

As Pastor Dick prepared for the meeting to be held later that evening, he began reminiscing about simpler days when the church nucleus was much smaller. He smiled to himself as he thought about the joy of having his entire family (Maddy, the girls and Daniel) working at his side. It had been a few months since he had spoken with Daniel and he found himself thinking about him, wondering what he was doing. Unbeknown to him, Chelsea had not divulged to him that she had been secretly keeping in touch with Daniel on a regular basis.

Before that fatal Tuesday when eleven of his church members had died, Pastor Dick received a call to come to the rehab center where Chelsea was receiving treatment. He had always felt a sense of guilt from Deacon Schmidt having lost his life because he had not facilitated the Bible study on that evening. He had not given much thought to him and the girls being called to the rehab center or why the entire staff seemed surprised to see him. It suddenly occurred to him that

Chelsea was incapable of making any special requests and the likelihood of the staff calling him on her behalf was also unlikely.

"Daniel!" he thought, pounding his fist on his desk.

Chelsea was standing just outside his door when she heard him shouting Daniel's name.

"Daddy, are you alright?" she asked.

"Not really!" her dad answered.

"Is there something I can help you with?"

"No, sweetheart, nothing at all!" he said.

"I heard you calling out Daniel's name."

"Yes, you did! And let me make it very clear to you, you are not to have any contact with him! He lives a very dangerous life and I don't want you anywhere near him! Have I made myself clear?"

"But dad!"

"But nothing, honey. I do not want you to have any contact with Daniel, for the safety and protection of our family!" Pastor Dick said.

"Yes, sir." Chelsea replied.

Pastor Dick quickly changed the subject to something more pleasant.

"Listen, Chelsea, I need to get ready for the board meeting this evening. Were you able to get all the quotes from the contractors for the meeting tonight?

"I have to get one or two more and we'll be all set." Chelsea said.

"Great! Now, would you mind closing the door behind you as you leave?" he said, smiling at her.

"Sure dad."

———

Deacon Menders loved the church and his Pastor. In fact, he regarded Pastor Dick as a very dear friend and the absolute best person for the job. However, with all the turn of events he had become increasingly concerned with the pastor's now marred and fragile personality. He often heard Pastor Dick preaching about forgiveness but he did not like the spirit that rested on him after the loss of Ms. Maddy, the church members and his son.

Deacon Menders decided to swing by the makeshift church at the school to check in on his friend. Upon his arrival, Chelsea greeted him warmly, which was easy considering how nice a man he was. Both her maternal and paternal grandparents had died when Chelsea was very young. In many ways, Deacon Menders was the grandfather she never knew. Because of it, she found it extremely easy to talk with him.

"Well hello, Ms. Chelsea! How's the Pastor today?"

"Good day to you, Deacon. Pastor is fine. Do you have a minute?" asked Chelsea.

"I always have time for you, Ms. Chelsea. I had nothing to do today, so I thought I would pop by and say hello."

"Deacon, when have you not had something to do?" Chelsea said jokingly.

They both chuckled.

"Deacon, do you mind if we go into the boardroom to talk? Pastor is busy getting ready for a meeting tonight and I have something I need to talk to you about," Chelsea said, closing the door behind her.

"Deacon, I have never kept anything from my dad before but awhile back I found Daniel. Do you remember my brother, Deacon?"

"Yes, I do," Deacon Menders said.

"Well, with all the things that happened to our family, I felt led to visit Danny in the hospital to express my gratitude and appreciation for him finding me and to let him know that I had forgiven him."

"I understand you wanting to thank him but I'm not sure I understand the forgiving part," Deacon Menders replied.

"Deacon, Jesus encourages us through the word to forgive others. When I was going through rehab, I learned that personal healing begins when a person learns how to forgive themselves, as well as all the people who has done them wrong. So, I made it my mission to find Daniel. He had been admitted to Amityville Hospital shortly after his last encounter with my dad. He had been shot a couple times but the doctors were only able to successfully remove one bullet. The other bullet is still in him and it's alive."

Chelsea continues. "A passerby found Danny slumped over his steering wheel in the layby and called an ambulance for him. But by the time he arrived at the hospital, the doctor's discovered that the live bullet had exploded and was now traveling through his blood stream. Because he also had a heart condition, the ruptured bullet caused a lot of damage. So much damage that they couldn't operate. So, for now, Danny is confined to a bed and the doctor said his days are numbered. "So, when I saw Danny, I told him that I was thankful that he had found me and that I knew that he never meant to hurt mommy; even though his actions and the people he was connected to caused mommy's death. We had a long discussion afterwards and he accepted the Lord as his personal savior. Danny's going to be released from the hospital as soon as the doctors can determine how to keep him stable. One wrong move and Danny could die."

Deacon Menders listened intently before responding: "Chelsea, what is it that you really want to ask me?"

"Well, today I heard my dad shouting out Daniel's name. When I entered his office to see if there was anything I could help him with, he became defensive. No one in the family can even mention Danny's name without my father exploding. My sisters and I talk privately about Danny all the time. Once, little Maddy asked my dad about Danny and he nearly snapped her head off. How do I explain to my dad that I have been visiting Danny on a regular basis, to the point of assisting him while he is bedridden? I have never ever kept secrets from my dad but I'm afraid of what he might do if he finds out. So, what do I do?"

"Chelsea, I want you to take out your phone and read aloud Colossians 3:9-10." Deacon Menders said.

Chelsea did as he asked and began reciting the passage.

"Do not lie to each other, since you have taken off your old self with its practices and have put on the new self, which is being renewed in knowledge in the image of its Creator."[22]

---

[22] Colossians 3:9-10, NIV

"I don't know if I have the courage to tell him. I'm afraid," Chelsea said.

"Chelsea, you are the bravest, most compassionate person I know. Plus, you "can do all things through Christ [23] with His help and strength". Was there anything else you wanted to discuss with me?"

"No Deacon. Thank you for always being there for me."

The two shook hands and Deacon Menders headed towards Pastor Dick's office. As he slowly walked towards the pastor's office, he thought to himself, "That child has a true compassionate heart," which put a smile on his face. Knocking on the door, Deacon Menders enters Pastor Dick's office:

"Good day, sir! May I have a minute of your time?"

"Hey Deacon Menders! I always have time for you. Please, come on in. I was just about to call you to remind you of the meeting tonight and to make sure we are operating from the same page. Have a seat, Deacon!" Pastor Dick replied.

As friendly as Pastor Dick was towards his friend, Deacon Menders could sense a heavy presence in the room.

"Pastor, we need to talk," he said humbly.

---

[23] Philippians 4:13, NIV

"Is everything alright, Deacon?"

"You tell me, Pastor. Is everything alright with you?"

"Funny you should ask that because I am struggling with something."

"Ok, so what is it?"

"Well, I was sitting here thinking about all the events that occurred prior to the church when something occurred to me. When I got the call to come to the rehab because Chelsea wanted to see me and her sisters, it never occurred to me that Chelsea was too out of it to have made such a request. Plus, the entire nursing staff seemed genuinely surprised to see us."

"So, what's your point?" Deacon Menders asked.

"Daniel!" he yelled with great disdain.

"So, are you saying that Daniel is your point?"

"Exactly! That boy has been nothing but trouble ever since he got his voice back! Maddy and I tried to pour all our love into him and what did we get for it? Him killing my Maddy and eleven of our church members! He better not step foot in my presence ever again! If I ever see him again, I will probably…"

"Careful, Pastor." Deacon Menders said.

"Pastor, who really killed Maddy and the church members?"

"What do you mean who killed them? How can you ask me a question like that after everything I just told you? Daniel did this!"

"Pastor, Revelation 13:7 reminds us that the beast "was given power to wage war against God's holy people and to conquer them. And it was given authority over every tribe, people, language and nation. The last part of Revelation 13:10 says, "this calls for patient endurance and faithfulness on the part of God's people."

"So, Pastor, I ask you again, "Who killed Maddy and the church members?"

Pastor Dick cupped his face as tears began to run down his cheeks:

"Every Believer is supposed to be a student of the Word of God. If we can't identify satanic forces and their impact on the people of God, then who can? Furthermore Pastor, how do we teach, preach and demonstrate patient endurance and faithfulness if not through our example?"

"Satan used Daniel to wreak havoc on you, your family and the people of God. So, I ask you to seriously reconsider your claims against Daniel. We have been called to teach and preach the Word of God but it is equally important for us to live a life that is reflective of Jesus Christ. None of us are exonerated from being tempted by the forces of darkness."

"Pastor, I am personally concerned about you. You preach and teach sound doctrine but your heart has become like stone."

Pastor Dick began crying uncontrollably.

"Pastor Dick, look at me and listen to what I am telling you. You must learn to forgive yourself and Daniel. Whether you facilitated the Bible study on that dreadful Tuesday or not, the outcome would have been the same because the events had already been set into motion. You cannot hold yourself responsible for something you had no control over. Think about it, you tragically lost your wife, Ms. Maddy (albeit very painfully) through Daniel's actions but your daughter was also restored to you because of Daniel's actions as well. Chelsea left home with a heart of stone but returned with a heart of compassion. We can build the biggest and most sophisticated church in the world but if our hearts are not right, then none of it really matters."

"Though I speak with the tongues of men and of angels, and have not charity, I am become as sounding brass, or a tinkling cymbal."[24]

With that said, Deacon Menders quietly excused himself and eased out of the room. Convicted by his own misgivings and shortcomings, Pastor Dick sat in his office crying and

---

[24] 1 Corinthians 13:1

shaking his head out of pure anger. There was no question that the words of his respected friend and colleague had pierced his soul. Now, the ball was in his court. Either Pastor Dick would choose to align himself with the character of God or not. Only time would tell.

SANCTUM OF TIME

There was an inner excitement after my conversation with Chelsea. The conversation was long but it felt like my emotional and spiritual life had taken a turn for the better. "I just need to get up and start moving," I thought to myself, as Dr. Westmund entered the room:

"Hey Doc! With that solemn look on your face, I know it must be good news!"

"Well, Mr. Schmartz, we will be releasing you tomorrow," said Dr. Westmund.

"By the look on your face, I knew you had to be cooking up something."

"Mr. Schmartz, I am releasing you on one condition: You absolutely must minimize your movements. During your stay here, we have been monitoring you and you appear to be responding very well to treatment. Therefore, I have arranged for you to be discharged by wheelchair only."

"Ok, doc. You had me scared for a minute. I thought you were going to give me some really bad news. I mean, my pride may be scarred leaving in a wheelchair but I will get over it."

"Mr. Schmartz, you are not understanding me. If you want to live, you need to be confined to a wheelchair for the rest of your life. So, no, the wheelchair it is not just to transport you out of the hospital but you will be confined to it."

"A wheelchair?" I thought. "I am Daniel Ophillon Schmartz, II, a fourth-generation descendant of a line of Corporals and Sergeants. I have never engaged in fighting wars for my country but I have fought the wars of an accepting culture that embraces conflict as something normal. This type of war has become an integral part of a warped phenomenon. And because of it, my world has become a closed book—a book defined by a life that is confined to a wheelchair. Nothing more can be added. My life has been stifled by my own actions. I may have salvation but I will forever be a war baby."

"Mr. Schmartz, do you have anyone we can call to assist you with your transition or do you need some time to think about it?"

"Yeah, I need time to think." I responded.

As Dr. Westmund left the room, my mind became flooded with questions that I had no answers to. I could not help but start crying, not because of self-pity but conviction. I felt convicted of all the things I had done and all the lives I had affected through my foolish actions. I wish I could turn back the hands of time but it was not within my power.

**The trajectory of time provides a sanctum
for all who respect it.**

"Nurse! Nurse Nelda! Can you do me a favor? Nurse? Anybody?"

Nurse Nelda did not answer but a familiar voice did.

"Hey Bro! I've been here so much. So, nurse Chelsea here! How can I assist you Mr. Schmartz?" Chelsea said giggling.

I needed a smiling friendly face about now.

"Hey Chelsea, how goes it?"

"It goes fine."

"You're awfully chipper today," I said.

"Yes, I am! Yesterday, I had a chat with Deacon Menders. Do you remember him?"

"Of course, I remember him! He's still alive? Wow, he must be 100 years old by now!"

"You are so rude, Danny. No, he's eighty and still kicking!"

"I've been feeling the weight of the world lately. Dad has forbidden us to mention your name let alone talk to you; and heaven help me if he should find out that I have been visiting you!"

"And you're happy about that?"

"No, silly. I'm happy because Deacon Menders encouraged me to be honest and talk to dad about everything, including your salvation. And you know what? I think I can do it. So, tonight's the night."

"Well, good luck with that one. What do you have planned for tomorrow?"

"Nothing much," Chelsea replied.

"Great, can you come by? I'm being discharged tomorrow."

"That's awesome!" Chelsea shouted.

"I need you to take care of some business for me. I'm going to have to make a lot of changes to adjust to my new lifestyle. I'll give you my banking details in a minute."

"Sounds intriguing. What do you need me to do?"

"Well for starters, I need a new place. Can you find me one in Amityville?" I asked.

"Amityville? You're moving back home? How exciting!" Chelsea said, unable to not stop grinning.

"Yup, I need to relocate. Dr. Westmund said that I need to be confined to a wheelchair, so I need a house that's handicap accessible. Can I leave all that up to you to handle for me?"

"Sure, Danny, I can do that. So, let me get this straight. You're getting discharged tomorrow and you want me to get you set up by when?"

"Tomorrow you silly goose!" Danny said while laughing.

"I'm teasing you, Chelsea! How about we schedule everything to happen by the end of next month. That'll give you at least six weeks to get everything done. Will that work for you?"

"Of course. With Christ all things are possible!" Chelsea said, rolling her eyes.

"Oh, and one last thing. Hurry up and have that conversation with dad. I'll need your help in getting to church the first Sunday of next month. I want to see dad and ask for his forgiveness and blessings."

"I'm so on this," said Chelsea.

The two of them high-fived each other before Chelsea left.

———————

It's three o'clock in the morning and the phone rings at Deacon Menders house. He turns on his little night lamp and answers:

"Hello, Deacon Menders here."

"Deacon, we are so sorry to call you at this hour but there has been a serious accident and we need you to keep Pastor's family in prayer." Sis. Schmidt says.

"I can do that but wouldn't it be best if I simply came to the hospital?"

"I think it would be better if we had Deacon Sanderman come by and pick you up. Don't you agree?"

"Ok, that'll be fine. I'll get ready." Deacon Menders said.

After Chelsea left the hospital, she approached her dad that evening and asked if they could talk. Reluctantly, Pastor Dick agreed. As for Chelsea, well let's just say that she had a very honest and open conversation with her father.

"Dad, you know that I have never kept anything from you, right?" Chelsea said.

"I guess so," he said.

"Well, I need you to know that I have been in contact with Danny ever since you told him you didn't want him to come near our family. Dad, Daniel is every much a part of this family as me, Melissa, Courtney and little Maddy are. And if mommy were here she would agree."

Chelsea did not expect the response she received.

"Chelsea Therault, you have no idea what your mother would have approved of!" Pastor Dick yelled. "That monster, Daniel, ordered a hit on your mother and this church. I will be damn if I am going to sit here and have you talk to me about that demon. He's evil and he has the ability to bring hell here on earth!"

Overhearing the yelling between Chelsea and her dad, Melissa, Courtney and little Maddy came running into the kitchen. In unison, they all called out:

"Daddy, what's going on!"

"Go back to your room," he shouted, "you don't need to hear any of this!"

"But daddy we do! We are a family and Danny is a part of our family! You taught us about forgiveness daddy and you have to let go of all this bitterness and hatred!" the three of them said.

Little did the three of them know that their dad was going through a grieving process. To deal with that grief, Pastor Dick had started drinking shortly after the death of their mother. Being the oldest, Chelsea was aware of her father's state of mind but had never let on to the others how he was or what had precipitated it. Chelsea could smell a hint of liquor on his breath but chose to ignore it and simply speak to him concerning the things on her heart.

Pastor Dick's life had fallen apart. He missed his wife Maddy. In his mind, the church had lost eleven of their members because of his irresponsibility in not facilitating the Bible study on that dreadful Tuesday. Instead of trusting in the Jesus he preached, Pastor Dick found solace in his new best friend, Johnnie Walker Black.

Even after his conversation with Deacon Menders, his heart was still hardened. Forgiveness was something he was not willing to embrace, even if it meant healing him and his family. The only thing he could see or think of was Daniel.

"I hate Daniel for what he has done to our family." Pastor Dick yelled.

"Daddy!" How can you say that?" Chelsea said with tears in her eyes.

"Say what?"

"You actually hate Daniel?"

"No, that's not what I said! I mean, that's not what I meant to say anyway."

Chelsea and her sisters stood side-by-side crying over the bitterness and hatred spewing from their father. Chelsea looked towards heaven, pleading:

"Oh God! Lord please help us! Daddy what has happened to you?"

"God? God? You are calling on the God that I have served for most of my life? The God that took your mother from me? You are calling on that God?" There ain't no God!" Pastor Dick yelled as he threw the empty Johnnie Walker bottle against the wall.

"Where are my keys?" he yelled.

The girls had never seen their father in such a state.

"Daddy, you are not in a good position to drive. Let me fix you some coffee, please daddy!"

"Coffee? I don't want any damn coffee!" he said, searching for his car keys.

Courtney remained at Chelsea's side. Maddy spotted the keys, peeking out from under some magazines on the table. She quietly went over and retrieved them. In his rage, he saw Maddy with his keys and with one single stroke slapped her, causing her tiny little body to ricochet off the wall. Little Maddy lay motionless against the wall. Both Melissa and Courtney screamed:

"Maddy, Maddy," they yelled, running over to aid their little sister.

"Daddy! Daddy what have you done!" screamed Chelsea.

Pastor Dick looked at all that was before him and cried out, "Oh God, what have I done?"

Crying profusely, he ran out of the house and jumped into his car.

Alcohol is a spirit. That spirit has the authority to stimulate merciless behavior.

"Melissa call 911!" Chelsea screamed as she ran to Maddy.

Maddy had a terrible gash on her head and her breathing was labored. Chelsea immediately began to pray:

"I come against every demonic spirit that is trying to uproot and upset this family and household, in the name of Jesus. Lord God, be with my daddy. You know his heart and how he has served you faithfully. Please forgive him Lord and please help our family and heal little Maddy. In Jesus' name I pray, Amen."

Shortly after Chelsea concluded the prayer, the paramedics arrived.

"Melissa, Courtney and I will ride in the ambulance with Maddy. I need you to take the car and drive carefully behind us. Melissa, did you hear me!" Chelsea screamed.

Somewhat in a daze, Melissa said, "Yes, Chelsea, I hear you."

Unknown to everyone else, Melissa was sensing death knocking at little Maddy's door. After the ambulance left, she fell to her knees and began to pray:

"Dear Lord, I know you have mommy up there with you. As you are about to receive Maddy, I ask that you help her to not feel any pain and that you would receive her with open arms. Mommy, Maddy is coming. Please look out for her. I love you and miss you so much. Lord, thank you for answering prayer, Amen."

The hospital was a fifteen-minute ride from the house. Chelsea watched as the paramedics performed CPR on little Maddy trying to save her life. Seven minutes into the ride little Maddy died. Chelsea and Courtney sat motionless, paralyzed from the shock of seeing the lifeless body of an innocent blonde-haired angel. Chelsea knew her little sister was gone but she held on to Courtney tightly in desperate consolation.

Melissa was not far behind but purposely did not travel the same route as the ambulance to the hospital. Instead, she was lead to drive to the Amityville Cemetery where her mother was laid to rest. A thirty-five-minute ride from the house, the roads to the cemetery were unusually dark. Melissa had not been driving that long so Chelsea's advice in 'driving cautiously behind the ambulance' made a lot of sense. She was simply driving cautiously in a different direction. Twenty minutes into the ride on Cemetery Road, Melissa noticed a series of red lights flashing in the distance. The lights looked strangely familiar as though a horrible accident had occurred off Cemetery Road.

"Oh God!" Melissa cried out. "Please don't let that be daddy."

As Melissa pulled over she called 911 to report the accident, advising the operator that she was on Cemetery Road with her emergency lights flashing. Melissa then left her vehicle to investigate. Recognizing her daddy's car, she screamed: "Daddy!"

Melissa immediately called Chelsea screaming in the phone: "It's daddy, it's daddy!" Then her phone went dead. She had a tendency of forgetting to charge her cell phone. Tonight proved to be the one night that she should have charged it. When the ambulance came, Melissa jumped back into her car and followed it to the hospital.

———

Deacon Menders finally arrived at the hospital and was greeted by Sis. Sheila.

"Deacon Menders! I'm so glad you are here!" she said. "Let me bring you up to speed on what's going on."

"What's going on with Pastor?" Deacon Menders asked.

"It's not Pastor, its little Maddy!"

"Little Maddy? But I thought you said there was a serious accident?"

"Yes, Deacon, there was. I don't know all the particulars but little Maddy died this evening on the way to the hospital!"

"Oh my, where is Pastor Dick now?"

"I'm not sure."

Both Deacon Menders and Sis. Sheila were visibly shaken. Neither of them could imagine this family suffering more tragedy than what they had already experienced but it was extremely important for cooler heads to prevail at a time like this.

"Where is Chelsea, Melissa and Courtney?" Deacon Menders asked.

"They are in the waiting area."

"Take me to them, please."

Deacon Menders entered the emergency room area and saw three lost little girls, traumatized and broken beyond what anyone could imagine.

"Chelsea, Melissa and Courtney," he called out gently.

Hearing his voice, they simultaneously looked up and rushed towards him.

"No, no girls. Just stay where you are. I'm here now."

Deacon Menders embraced the three of them, cuddling and caressing them in his arms.

"Deacon, we don't know how our dad is!" Chelsea said. "Why is this happening to us? Are we under some sort of attack?"

Deacon Menders responded, "I don't know the answer to that but let us pray."

"Our Father which art in heaven, Hallowed be thy name. Thy kingdom come. Thy will be done in earth, as it is in heaven. Give us this day our daily bread. And forgive us our debts, as we forgive our debtors. And lead us not into temptation, but deliver us from evil: For thine is the kingdom, and the power, and the glory, forever. Amen. "[25]

They all said, "Amen." Danny's vision suddenly became vivid to Chelsea and all she could do is pray that it was not so. About thirty minutes later, Sis. Schimdt entered the waiting room with a horrifying look on her face, revealing the one thing Chelsea feared the most. She looked up at Sis. Schmidt, sobbing ever so softly:

"No! Not my daddy!"

Sis. Schmidt shook her head in affirmation that Pastor Dick had died.

---

[25] Matthew 6:9-13, NIV

FINAL WORDS

The long-awaited day for Danny to leave the Amityville Hospital had finally come. He had been waiting for Chelsea to show up but she never did. Worried that something might have happened to her, Danny made some calls until he finally reached Chump.

"Hey man, long time no hear!"

"Hey Danny, how you doing?" responded Chump.

"Well, I'm calling because I need a ride. I'm getting discharged today!"

"Sweet! I can be there in about twenty minutes!"

"Hey, it's a thirty-minute drive so don't get caught by the man for my sake!"

"Ok. I'll get there as soon as I can."

It was unlike Chelsea to not follow through on her word. The more Danny thought about where she was the more worried he became. Had she forgotten and simply become too busy to remember? Had something tragically happened to her? Had she talked with her father and was somehow discouraged from coming?

Claim and enjoy the benefits of being a child of the Most High God, for they are priceless!

Before Danny could entertain another thought he heard a familiar voice in a clap of thunder telling him to write these words:

War is an intrinsic and inflammatory position for acquisition, whether it involves a retrieval of personal possession by force, a position of headship, or to determine a tactic to undergird the economy. War can present a contest carried out by force of a nation against or for another nation, and leadership against headship bringing with it many casualties to include both the guilty and the innocent.

War is an authority to promote the sovereignty of God to mankind for the protection of a chosen group of people. War establishes a place of humility between God and humanity. War is beneficial to secure and redirect rightful ownership while displacing those that operate in corruption.

War is evitable, yet it will stretch beyond nations, nestling itself within the bowels of one's persona as it matriculates weaponry of mass destruction. The destruction that will cause the strongest of personalities to submit to mediocrity, a family to turn against each other, and an institution of affluence to exploit its patrons.

War is without prejudice, for it is an action fueled by the personalities of those that will implement the initiative. It can engulf the actions of a subtle and brilliant mind that is yet to be demarcated by the values and truth determined by parental, educational and spiritual disclosure.

War transcends in a natural progression, arresting the culture that embraces it as a means to an end. A cultural understanding that embraces conflict as a position of harmony is an eccentric view and one that gains an unearned support by a premise of artificial entitlement.

If we surrender to the wars that surround us it will consume us. It will make us compromise who we are and who we are predestined to be. Many have been caught up in the war and perhaps it feels like it is impossible to get out but I found a way out. My history will say that I am a war baby but my newfound future says that I am a child of the Most High God. The war I choose to represent is warding off every demonic force that aims to consume mankind.

Just as I finished writing, Chump walked through the door. It was good seeing my old friend. The two of us drove in silence as we reminisced over all that had transpired; and knowing that it still was not over yet. Once we arrived at the apartment, I dropped off my belongings and asked Chump to swing me by the Wyandanch Foster Home so I could take care of some unfinished business.

Riding through the halls of the foster home at twenty-four years old, I noticed many things had changed. The administration had changed and was led by a Baptist youth minister. The whole atmosphere of the house felt different. Maybe because I was different. There were a lot of new faces there. The old superintendent had retired, and so the staffing looked different also. I introduced myself to the youth minister and gave him my background and my connection to the facility. I asked if he would round up the thirty or so young men that were residing there and he agreed. I waited patiently with Chump by my side for everyone to gather.

"My name is Daniel Ophillon Schmartz II, a fourth-generation descendant of Corporals and Sergeants. I never served in the army, navy or Special Forces. But I am a war baby, saved by the grace of God. There is no need for you to engage in war. The war that you facilitate hurts, kills, steals and destroys those you love and that love you. Know that it is the work of satan. Because of the war I chose to fight, I now speak to you from the confines of this wheelchair. Look at me closely and hear what I am saying to you. Should you have to fight any war, fight the war against mediocrity, as it is that evil that will consume your soul and personal potential. To be successful in your battles of life, become strong in the Lord and in the strength of His might and dress for battle. You must wear the proper artillery:

Therefore, "I implore you to put on the full armor of God, so that you will be able to stand firm against the schemes of the devil. Gird your loins with His truth; put on the breastplate of righteousness, on your feet put on the Gospel of Peace. When the war really kicks in, take up your shield of faith that will extinguish every firing dart that will be hurled at you from the devil, always wear your helmet of salvation and never, ever leave home without the sword of the Spirit, which is the word of God."[26]

Young men, I am neither proud nor upset of how my life turned out. I had to look at the man in the mirror and conclude, either I stay in this place or I get out. Before I was discharged from the hospital where I spent at least two months the second time around, I penned these words:

If we give in to the wars around us, it will consume us; make us compromise who we are and who we are predestined to be. Many have been caught up in the war, but I found a way out. My history will say that I am a war baby, but my newfound future says, I'm a child of the Most High God and the war I choose to represent is warding off every demonic force that aims to consume mankind.

I thanked the Youth Pastor for allowing me to have time with the residents. I also thanked Chump, but told him I had to do one last thing.

Chump responded, "Anything you need, man!"

As he got me back to my apartment, I told him, "Tomorrow I need to go to Amityville."

"Man, you have been going none stop since you got out of the hospital. You need to rest." Chump declared.

"I'll rest when I die," I said. "See you tomorrow."

---

[26] Ephesians 6:14-17, NIV

When I woke up the next day, I really did not feel my best. Actually, I felt really bad. So, I looked up to heaven and asked God for one more day and to allow me to get to Amityville.

While I was preparing, I heard in the clap of thunder: "My son, I am calling you to me."

At that same time, there was a knock on the door. It was Chump.

"You ready, man?" he asked.

"Yup!" I answered, as I reached for the notes the Holy Spirit had inspired me write before leaving the hospital.

I looked at Chump and said, "Look man if anything should happen to me, I need you to get this note to Pastor Dick and tell Ms. Chelsea that I'm so sorry."

"Ok, but you are freaking me out!" said Chump.

"Man, I'm cool. Just promise me you'll do that."

"I got you man," said Chump.

As we went out the apartment door I knew that I would not be back. I put all my affairs in order, leaving everything I had to Chelsea, Melissa, Courtney and Maddy. I could not wait to see them.

"Oh yeah, on the way I'm going to have to stop to fill up the car, cool?" Chump stated.

"Yeah that's alright. Like where am I going to go? Hey, what you really up to?" I asked.

"Nothing man. After what happened to Pete and everybody, I had to get out. I've been living on the low side, if you know what I mean," Chump responded.

"Really," I commented.

"Yeah and what you said yesterday at the foster home, like really hit a nerve with me. It's like we still have to fight but that salvation thing…like man, Danny, you've really changed. I mean we used to tease you 'cause of the church thing but like, I will never forget how you rallied us together before the big blow out at Pete's; and like, how in the midst of war you prayed for us! Man, that was deep!" Chump said.

"Well, Chump, salvation can be yours too." I stated.

"Really, like how?" asked Chump.

"Well usually when we pray we close our eyes. But since you're driving I would prefer if we did the prayer with your eyes open and I'll close mine for the both of us, deal?"

We both chuckled.

"Yeah, that'll be some news. Two men found in the ditch holding hands. Nah, that ain't going to happen!" chided Chump.

"Ain't no holding hands going on here!" I laughed. "So, let's pray. Repeat these words after me, Chump." I said.

"Dear Lord, I admit that I am a sinner. I have done and still do so many things that I know does not please you. I have lived my life for myself only and, in the process, have hurt many people that I love, especially you. I am so sorry and I repent of all my sins and shortcomings. I ask you Lord to please forgive me. I believe that you died on the cross for me to save me. You did what I could not do for myself. I come to you now and ask you to take control of my life. I give my life to you. From this day forward, I ask that you help me to live every day for you in a way that pleases you. Thank you, Lord and I ask these things in Jesus' name. Amen."

"Hey man, thanks." Chump said.

"You're a good guy and perfect timing because there's a gas station up ahead."

"Hey Chump, don't forget to give that envelope to Chelsea for me and, I almost forgot, tell her I left something on the table at the apartment for her"

"Ok, man, you're getting weird and stuff again. I'll make sure she gets the message."

Chump went into the gas station to pick up a couple of items for the road. Before Chump returned, I heard the voice in a clap of thunder again:

"It's time, Daniel. It's time."

When Chump got back to the car he noticed Daniel slumped over in the car.

"Somebody help! Someone please call 911!"

Chump slid down the side of his car and started weeping. His longtime friend Danny was no longer among the living. He had died at the tender age of twenty-four, which was all too soon for his liking.

The processional was overwhelming. There in the Amityville High School Gymnasium were three caskets of varying sizes. The little one held Maddy's body. Next to her was my dad, Pastor Dick, and next to him was Daniel. All of them gone too soon. Chump had given me the letters from Daniel. He left all his possessions to the four of us, Melissa, Courtney, Maddy and me. Deacon Menders nudged me ever so gently:

"Chelsea, it's your turn to speak to the waiting congregation."

Chelsea looked out and saw the many lives touched by those represented in the three caskets. There was no standing room in the gym. People from all walks of life were present. She did not know what to say. As she looked down at Melissa, Melissa looked up at her with such strength and unmovable faith. Suddenly, Chelsea heard what sounded like a clap of thunder. She turned around and looked at all the deacons and those sitting on the pulpit but no one budged. She looked back at Melissa who was holding Courtney's hand and nodding at her head in affirmation that she had heard the clap of thunder too. Chelsea reached for her Bible and in it was the last thing that Danny had written. She cleared her throat and looked out at the waiting congregation.

> For all who have gathered here today, thank you on behalf of my sisters Melissa, Courtney and myself. We will never understand the intrinsic and total movement of war but what I have learned is that it can consume both the innocent and the guilty. It can disrupt the social rhythms of society. It can guide us away from what we know is right or it can propel us in the most powerful trajectory towards greatness.
>
> We can place blame on the vindictive colloquy hidden behind a teasing gesture. We can blame it on a lack of parental teaching and guidance or we can blame it on a past encounter. Know that only you can command your destiny! As believers, we have been given the proper artillery. When/if we choose to fight, we must put on the full armor of God so we can stand firm against the evil schemes of the devil.
>
> Knowing that we have this armor, let us gird our loins with His truth, putting on the breastplate of righteousness while covering our feet with the Gospel of peace. When war really kicks in, let us take up the shield of faith that can extinguish every fiery dart hurled against us by the devil. Let us protect our minds by covering our heads with the helmet of

salvation; and never, ever leave home without the sword of the Spirit, which is the word of God.'[27]

Church, family and dear friends, I stand before you to remind you that God has called us to fight but it is not the fight or warfare of men but of God and His Kingdom. To fight is to stand strong in solidarity, combating demons of mediocrity and self-centeredness so that as a people we will bond into the spirit of greatness.

As oddly strange as my brother Danny's life was, he held to the philosophy that he was always standing at the doorway of two possible futures and choices—mediocrity and opportunity. Between the two there was war. A war that will cause even the strongest person to surrender to inferior characteristics. Danny believed that war is a reality of life.

One of the greatest sermons my dad ever preached from this very pulpit and the thought I want to leave with you today is this: *Find Value While In The Valley.* I stand here a living witness that there is value in every valley experience. Those of you who may be living in a war or just read my brother's story, hopefully realize that he discovered his purpose and value by listening to the voice of God in the claps of thunder. In honor of my brother, Danny, I leave you with his final words—the words that he wrote just before he died after listening to the voice in the claps of thunder:

---

[27] Ephesians 6:14-17, NIV (Paraphrased)

If we give into the war around us, it will consume us. It will make us compromise and forfeit who we are and what we are predestined to be. Those who are caught up in war believe there is no way out but I found a way out. My history suggests that I am a War Baby and I accept that I am. But my newfound faith and future declares that I am a child of the Most High God—one who has found the courage to stand against all forms of evil, by fighting the good fight of faith." **— Daniel (Danny) Ophillon Schmartz, II**